HEIST

Book Two

By: Carissa McIntyre

I would never, ever have come this far without so many incredible people around me, supporting me, cheering me on and helping me see this thing through. Thank you to every single one of you, you mean the world to me. Keep on being amazing.

Special thanks to:

My beautiful cover model: Jess Lynne

Male Model: Derek Emery

Cover art photographer: Absent Imagination Photography

absentimaginationphoto@gmail.com

Carissa McIntyre is a self-published author from Ontario Canada. Her work can be found at
www.ladymackpublishing.com
Publishing / all other inquiries may be sent to:
carissa.mcintyre@hotmail.ca

New Adult – Romance -Erotica

Heist
Book Two

Chapter One

Adam slides his hand slowly up Demi's tanned leg, along her slender thigh, his grip firm on her soft skin. He applies pressure with his fingertips and uses his palm to force her legs to part, opening her up, exposing her intimate places, causing her to moan in the quiet of the car. The skin on the back of her thighs sticks to the leather seat underneath her as she parts her legs; it is a hot, sticky Georgia night, even with the windows wide open and the breeze blowing through while they roll down the highway. It's almost pitch black out here, with no street lights or nearby city to light the way, the moon and the stars hidden by clouds, and only the occasional passing headlights break through the darkness in front of them as they travel.

Demi feels his fingertips trail along her thighs by the bottom of her short skirt, pulling on it, tugging it up to expose more of her thighs. As her legs part wider, she feels the heat reach the wetness between them, and she remembers then that she isn't wearing any panties anymore; she lost them somewhere on their last "rest" stop, which was anything but a rest. They still can't seem to keep their hands off each other, and every moment feels like something out of a sexually charged high school teenager's wet dream. The last few weeks have been a blur of driving across the country, fucking, laying on the beach, having sex, drinking, and making love. More kinky, crazy, sexual things have been crossed off her bucket list over the past few weeks with him than she'd ever even realized she'd had on there. They are very comfortable with each other, they've had an unexplainable chemistry ever since the farm house, and Demi is enjoying every moment in his company, getting to know him and getting comfortable with being together.

Adam's finger brushes along her clit, rubbing the head of it gently, making her jump and bringing her out of her thoughts and back to reality. She moans and leans back in her seat, fixing her seatbelt and reclining slightly, getting adjusted, as he rubs one finger slowly back and forth over her hard nub. She's having trouble concentrating on just getting comfortable in her seat, moaning and panting and moving under his touch, but he never even looks at her, eyes on the road the whole time, his other hand gripping the steering wheel tightly.

He knows her body well by now, knows all her sweet spots and what she likes and what makes her cry out in ecstasy. And he loves doing exactly that to her, he loves hearing her yell out for him as she cums. He slides his fingers down her wet folds, easing his way along as she adjusts herself again, hiking her skirt a bit higher and opening herself up even more to him on the passenger seat. Adam pushes two fingers deep inside her, and they slide in easily as she's so wet for him, soaking in her own juices.

Demi cries out as he enters her, arching herself back on the seat, giving him total access to her. She's in her own world now, completely oblivious to any passerby's, not even noticing any headlights that light up the car. Adam forces his fingers in and out of her quickly, pushing upwards, rubbing on her g-spot lightly, then pulls them out and rubs them all over her clit, coating her in her own wetness. She cries out again, clinging to the seat behind her, pushing her hips up to meet his touch. Moaning, aching, desperate for more. He slides his fingers back down again, pushing them deep inside her, wiggling them, and this time pushes his hand back so that his palm is still rubbing against her clit.

This sets her off, bringing her closer to an orgasm, and she begins to buck on the passenger seat, pressing against the floorboards with her feet, making little mewing sounds, grinding her hips against his hand. Her thighs squeeze him tightly as she fucks his hand now, in control, his fingers sliding in and out of her wet hole as she moves, juices leaking down between them. She grabs at the seat belt and the seat, clinging to anything, and moans his name, feeling herself getting closer and closer to climax.

Adam sneaks a glance away from the road to the seat beside him as he drives, and he can't help but groan out loud at the scene before him; Demi sprawled out in the passenger seat, grabbing at everything around her, grinding against his hand, basically finger fucking herself with his fingers, legs spread wide and skirt hiked up over her hips. No panties on. Her eyes are closed, her mouth open, crying out for him, begging for more.

He picks up speed, pushing his fingers harder and faster inside of her, thrusting them in deep in time with her hips, wiggling them around, feeling her silky walls tightening around him. She's so wet, so horny, he can hear his fingers sliding in and out of her tight pussy louder than the sounds of her cries of passion. And his hand is drenched in her juices. A few more rubs, with him applying pressure with the palm of his hand on her clit, push her over the edge; her thighs clench around his wrist tightly, pinning his hand against her as she cums all over his fingers, crying out, grabbing tightly at the seat, almost lifting herself off of it.

Her slippery pussy walls tighten around his fingers, almost milking him, as she throws herself around, saying his name, pulling at her seatbelt, eyes closed, legs holding him tightly. She orgasm's hard, pinning him like that for a few moments as she withers and moans.

He gently strokes her a few more times as she comes down, lightly sliding his fingers in and out while holding the rest of his hand steady, listening to her heavy breathing slowly calm down, eyes still on the road. That had been so hot, his own cock is throbbing in response in his pants.

Then he pulls his hand away and lets her relax for a few minutes, letting them both relax, as they continue to drive down the dark, deserted highway.

Chapter Two

As he drives, Adam watches her out of the corner of his eye while she settles back in her seat, getting comfortable again and relaxing after her orgasm. He's still rock hard in his pants, but his mind is all over the place tonight, and his erection won't last long; he had only temporarily used her as a distraction while they drove towards the next city in their plans. Except the problem was, this city isn't really part of their plans, it is part of his, and that is what has his mind in turmoil. She has no idea why they are heading the way they are heading, and he has yet to figure out how he's going to talk to her about it.

Nothing about their relationship, and whatever it is that they have been doing since the farmhouse, is "normal" in any sense of the word. But really, Adam thinks to himself, when you start off as your girlfriend's kidnapper, as a stranger who snatches her half naked in the dark, holding her hostage for days with a buddy to collect ransom on her, and then end up falling in love with her, how normal can you expect your relationship to be? Everything between them is excitement, fire, thrill, passion, lust, forbidden; it is everything that's almost too much, and then some more. It's been the most intense relationship of his entire life, and he wouldn't change a single moment.

And somehow, on top of all the crazy kinky sex, the fun, the exploration, the desperate need for each other, they had still found themselves traveling down a path of danger that had only started with the kidnapping and snowballed from there. Although, the first incident after they left the city together fell on Demi, and it was entirely an accident. The two of them had been having what was actually almost a real fight, and their first one, although ridiculously it was about where they should head next on their travels. Where they were going didn't even matter to Adam, not at that point, but once they had started debating it, and that had progressed into somewhat of an argument between them, seeing Demi get mad turned him on in a way he hadn't experienced with her yet.

So, Adam had let their fight escalate, even though it was a jerk move on his behalf, and he let her get all fired up while he got all turned on, finding amusement in the situation. At the same time, she pulled into the gas station they'd been passing and announced they were almost out of gas. She had gotten out to fill the tank while he went inside to get snacks and coffee, and he only paid for those as she was still pumping. When he came out, she kept right on going with their fight, not going inside to pay, not even really missing a stride in the argument. And she kept on going while she got back in the car and they drove off, feeling extremely heated with him, while he found himself on the verge of laughter, with an incredible hard-on.

A few minutes later into the argument, and a few more miles down the road, Adam interrupted her to ask if she'd remembered to stop bitching long enough to go in and pay for the gas, knowing at this point she damn well hadn't. He didn't say another word, and Demi hit the brakes and turned off at the next exit and drove until she found a side road. She had pulled over and parked, shutting off the engine, and then she simply sat there in silence and disbelief that she'd stolen gas, unsure what she should do next. Technically, this made her some sort of criminal, she thinks in a panic, doesn't it?

Demi sat in the driver's seat, gripping the steering wheel so tightly her knuckles were turning white, caught up somewhere between going back to pay for it, thoughts about being arrested, and the overall excitement of what she'd just done. She turned to look at him, and Adam caught the look in her eyes, wild and horny and uncertain. Still being turned on himself he wasted no time taking advantage of the moment, his cock still throbbing in his pants, aching for release. He had leaned over and kissed her deeply, unbuckling her seatbelt, and he'd pulled her over into his lap. He was desperate to be buried inside her, and she felt his cock pressing up against her the second she was on top of him.

She pulled back in excitement and disbelief at his horniness, and she asked him if her being a thief was a turn on. He had laughed and told her that maybe it was a little bit that and a little bit that he had loved watching her get mad while they fought. He told her she was bad, just like him. She was his bad girl. She wasn't sure exactly what to make of that, but her pussy throbbed in response to his words and she knew what the rest of her was thinking, so she leaned in and kissed him hard, forcing her tongue into his mouth, and pushed her body up against his in the seat, grinding herself into him.

They had shared some very hot sex in the car that evening, despite the crammed quarters, and being parked in public on the side of the road, both getting off on the thrill and excitement of everything that had come to pass between them in the last few days. Adam had only just gotten away with committing a kidnapping, not only leaving himself fairly rich, but winning over the woman he had kidnapped, then leaving everything they knew behind and making a run for it, and now here she was preforming a gas and go, which was totally unnecessary, but oh, so very exhilarating.

And for some reason, the gas and go that night ended up only being the beginning for them, both of them wanting more, wanting to see how far they could take it. From there, they had done a few small robberies at mom and pop stores, in different cities that they traveled through, and she shop lifted from a few malls, everything from jewelry to clothing and purses and scarves, just to take them. And every time afterwards, they had stopped somewhere, the side of the road, behind a building, in the car, a hotel, wherever they'd happened to be, and fucked each other silly, high on the experience and the thrill.

But, Adam thinks to himself, watching the occasional car pass by on the dark highway, lights illuminating the car as he drives, they've never done anything quite like what he's got planned for them next. He hasn't spoke to her about it at all, kept it to himself so far, he doesn't even know if she'll be ok with the idea, but he's taking them that way down the highway anyway. It's an opportunity for some real thrill and excitement, beyond anything they've experienced so far, and an almost perfect crime, that would leave them rich for a very, *very* long time.

He keeps quiet for a while, lost in his own thoughts of what could possibly lie ahead for them, and focused on getting them to the hotel before midnight, so they can have a chance to relax and get settled a bit before he talks to her about his plans. He doesn't know what to expect, but he knows that the small space of the car while they drive is not the place for that conversation.

Chapter Three

Now it's Demi's turn to watch Adam closely out of the corner of her eye over the last few dozen miles of the drive, although for all the good sneaking glances at him has done, she may as well have turned around in her seat and sat there gawking at him, he is so lost in his own thoughts. And she has noticed especially now that they've reached the hotel, he's become even more distant and quiet. Stone faced. And totally unreadable.

She is slowly noticing that about him; it doesn't appear easy for him to open up about certain things, or really anything at all, and when he has something on his mind, good or bad, he has a tendency to shut down completely, and shut her out. She had tried to question him a few times before they reached the hotel and checked themselves in, and tries again now, but she isn't getting much of a response from him, and so her mind begins to spiral out of her control. She tries to get her thoughts together now that they've checked into their room and she has a chance to get changed and freshen up, but once she starts thinking about everything, she can't stop. Quickly, she goes from being sexually satisfied and happy, to feeling overwhelmed and a mess.

Despite all the chemistry between them, Demi still finds herself feeling insecure and unsure about things more often than not, and almost all of the time it ends up being something ridiculous that she is hung up on. Relationships are new to her, especially one as intense and crazy as this one, and finding her footing alongside him as they go isn't always easy. Although, she thinks to herself, it might have been a bit easier if they weren't constantly traveling on the road with no fixed address, in crammed quarters, constantly in each other's space, living like Bonnie and Clyde, and were dating and moving in together like normal couples would be instead.

Looking at her, Adam can tell that Demi is getting all worked up in her head, which is only adding to the anxiety of what he's about to ask her, and he knows that he isn't helping the situation either. He takes a deep breath and stops pacing around the hotel room, walks over and opens the mini bar fridge and grabs himself a beer to calm his nerves a little bit. Then he walks over to the window with it and takes a few swigs, watching the cars passing by below, and the lights of the city late at night, willing his heart to stop racing. When he thinks he's ready, he turns to her and starts to talk.

"I've been thinking about another robbery we could do. A really big robbery, in someone's house, yet a really easy one, with a lot of jewels and possibly some money at stake. I got wind of it when I was talking with a buddy of mine and I think we could pull it off, especially with his help. It would be exciting as all hell." Now that he's said everything he needs to say, in one quick spiel, he shifts against the window frame nervously, holding his beer in his hand tightly, waiting for her reply.

Demi stares at him for a minute in disbelief; partly mad at herself for getting so worked up and letting her emotions run wild over absolutely nothing (and what else is new there) and partly mad at him, for springing his idea on her like this.

Clearly, he's put a lot more thought into it than anything else that they have gotten into so far, because everything else has been sporadic and thrilling and fun, and this was something he'd obviously been planning, and without her for at least a little while. And he had included someone else in on it too, at least a little bit. It was something that he had kept secret from her, for whatever reason. Given the nature of the start of their relationship, trust is something that she is terrified about, and desperately wants between them. This is not helping that bond at all.

She tries to tell him as much, but she's so emotional and already so worked up from earlier, that she can already hear her voice crack with anger and tears before she's hardly started speaking, and she hates herself for it. That fuels the anger that she's feeling too, and before she knows it, they've begun to fight. "I wasn't trying to lie to you." Adam starts to explain to her, interrupting her yelling, but she doesn't see it that way, and she's too hurt and too mad to keep arguing with him right now.

"To hell with it, with all of it," she yells at him, suddenly feeling overwhelmed, and overheated, ripping off and throwing the sweater she's wearing on the bed in a tantrum. She stalks over to the table and grabs her purse, throwing the strap over her shoulder in a huff. "I need a drink, and I don't need one here in this room with you. I'm going down to the bar, by myself. I need time to think." She doesn't even look at him while she says this, she just takes her keys alongside her purse and walks out, and she makes sure she slams the door behind her, letting him know that she's angry with him, even though she knows it's childish.

Demi walks down the hallway to the elevator in a whirlwind of thoughts and emotions, her head spinning and her hands shaking. She's still caught up in the fact that she feels lied to, and after everything that has happened between them in the past few weeks, that is the last thing that she wants to feel. The elevator seems to take forever to get to their floor, and she can't help but keep glancing down the hallway at their hotel room door, pacing from foot to foot, expecting him to come out after her at any moment. But he must have realized she was serious, because he never does chase her down, and after what seems like an eternity the elevator pings in front of her and finally opens.

She gets inside, already second guessing her decision to leave, but she knows she needs to clear her thoughts and get her head on straight, and exactly like she'd said, she's not going to be able to do that in there. Demi takes the lift down to the main level and wanders towards the bar and restaurant area that she'd seen was still open when they first checked in. She isn't sure if alcohol is the answer right now, but it definitely can't hurt anything.

Walking over to the bar, she pauses for a few moments to take in the scenery and the look of the place. It's modern, and well done, and she loves the paintings they have along the walls and the water and flower arrangements that are scattered amongst the corners, surrounded by mirrors. The sound of the flowing water, mixed with some light instrumental music, is quite soothing.

Demi walks to the bar and orders a drink, and when it arrives she takes it over to a table by the windows that overlook the city and sips it slowly while she lets her thoughts and her breathing and racing heart calm down. Everything has happened so fast between them, and everything seems to escalate and happen at such a fast pace, everything giving them such an exciting thrill, that it really doesn't surprise her that the few fights they seem to get themselves into happen in the same manner. They never seem to talk about anything before hand, they just act on a whim as they go, and deal with the aftermath later.

After the kidnapping, and after Adam had found her in the park across from the mall, things between them have begun developing in a quick blur. They hadn't been able to keep their hands off each other, or stay away from one another, not for a moment. Demi hadn't exactly been able to take him back to her house with her mother there, just in case, so they had gone to Adam's place for the night, even though he knew it was a huge risk. That only lasted one night, as Adam was far too much on edge to be there at all, let alone with her, and he knew it wasn't exactly keeping a low profile, so the next night they spent at a hotel, that he insistent they pay for with cash.

But paranoia still got to them both, even if it wasn't entirely unjustified, and by the end of the second day, Demi emptied out all the bank accounts and cards that she could get her hands on, liquifying it into cash, and told her mother she was going off on vacation for a while, just to do some traveling, to find herself again after everything that had happened. Then she packed a few bags of clothes and necessities and Adam did the same, and they filled the tank of her car, bought some snacks and hit the road.

With no destination in mind, and no real plans made, they simply drove; taking turns behind the wheel, talking, laughing, taking the time getting to know one another. The chemistry between them was intense, yet easy; conversations flowed naturally, and for hours, and just being in each other's company was enough right now. It was more than enough. It was almost the perfect honey moon stage and beginning to a relationship, if they left out how it started, and the fact that right now, they were living out of her car, and hotels, always on the go. With no daily life distractions, no real responsibilities and an abundance of money at their fingertips, they had ample time to really connect, and get to know one another as their relationship grew, as well as explore the world. It seemed perfect.

They went where they wanted, exploring places along the map they'd each wanted to see, and they learned a lot about each other as they went, especially being together all the time. And they were learning a lot about each other sexually as well. In such tight quarters, with the sexual chemistry between them so intense, they were eager to open up to each other, to learn and explore one another's bodies and desires. There were a few nights that they had spent out along the coast, laying under the stars, talking and fucking, just spending time together watching the sun come up, that were now some of the best nights of Demi's life, and memories she planned to keep forever.

All of those crazy connections between them, all of the excitement they were experiencing, all of the fun of the new, combined with the thrill of the illegal activities that they'd added into the mix, had made for a really wild few weeks, unlike anything that Demi had ever been through in her life, especially following the kidnapping. Everything was so chaotic and out of control already, could she really expect any kind of real normalcy within their relationship? And could she really blame Adam for wanting to take things one step further, like she had kept taking things one step further, just to see how much fun they could have, what they could get away with, and what they were ballsy enough to do? It wasn't as if Adam had just drove them right up to a house to rob someone and dumped it all on her either, with no notice, while they were acting like calm, law-biding citizens, and then just expected her to do something totally unheard of.

Demi sighs to herself, playing with the half empty drink glass in her hand, realizing she's probably had too many to drink by now, but she hadn't been paying attention. Her thoughts are a lot more settled though, and she feels calmer, which is all that she wanted to gain by leaving for a little while. At any point during their journey she could have called it quits, told him it was all too much, put the brakes on things and gone back to a normal life, but she hadn't. In fact, a lot of things she had encouraged or even instigated herself. She knows she doesn't really have a right to put any blame on Adam when a lot of the blame falls on her too. She owes him an apology for the way she reacted.

She finishes up her drink and pays her tab, feeling a little wobbly as she walks away from the bar and heads back through the lobby towards the elevators. She has definitely drunk more than she realized, having been so lost in thought she simply kept ordering them when the waiter came by. She takes a deep breath and lets it out slowly, trying to steady herself as she pushes the elevator button and waits for it to come down for her. She's ready to go upstairs and apologize, she just hopes Adam isn't too upset with her, or too drunk, to hear her out, or to talk about his plans with her.

Chapter Four

If the elevator going down seemed to take forever, going back up feels like it's taking an eternity and a day. It doesn't help that she is drunk now, and antsy to get back to the hotel room to talk things over with Adam, practically bouncing back and forth from foot to foot while she waits. She keeps fidgeting with the room key in her hand, watching the numbers at the roof of the lift change as it crawls ever so slowly to their floor. When it finally stops, and the doors open, she nearly stumbles out of the elevator into the hallway, a mixture of eagerness and drunkenness taking over her, anxious to get back to the room.

She makes it down the hallway and stands in front of their door for a moment, key shaking in her hand, still thinking, trying to get her thoughts and the world to stop spinning. Demi can hear faint music coming from inside the room, most likely from the TV, and her thoughts start racing; she wonders if Adam has been drinking too, if he's upset with her, if he will even want to talk things through right now. She wonders once more if leaving to calm down was a good idea, but she knows in her heart that it was. Nothing will get solved when they are both heated and not thinking clearly, all up in each other's faces like they were.

Taking a deep breath, she steadies herself and uses the room key to open the door. She slides it open hesitantly so that she doesn't startle him, but it doesn't matter anyway because she can tell as soon as she enters that he's not exactly in the room. She can see and hear him, out on the patio, singing along to the music, and he's clearly been drinking too, as he's waving a bottle around in his hand while he grooves to the song. Well, she thinks to herself, this could go one of two ways. Either he's drank himself into a calmer, more reasonable mood like she has, and now they can talk this all out, and maybe have some really hot make-up sex, or, alternatively, he's still angry and upset with her, and the alcohol he's consumed is only going to intensify that.

Demi knows she doesn't have much choice though; she is going to have to face him one way or another, so she takes another deep breath and slowly makes her way across the hotel room towards the balcony, dropping her purse and keys on the table as she goes. She gets to the patio door, which is still slightly opened, and slides it the rest of the way, stepping out into the night beside him, before shutting it almost all the way behind her, letting the music still flow out.

Adam is surprised to see her appear suddenly beside him. He's been so lost in thought, and drinking heavily himself, that he never heard or noticed her until she is right there next to him, startling him. His head is a mess, all his thoughts spinning out of control, and he doesn't even know what to say to her when he sees her there. He can tell that she's been drinking too, her eyes slightly glazed over, and her step swaying, and he no longer knows what her mood is like. He just wants to apologize to her and make everything right.

When Adam turns to look at her, Demi can see that he's not just drunk, he's tired and worn out too, and his eyes look heavy, like he's got a lot on his mind. She feels bad again for reacting the way that she did, especially after they had been driving for so long, and both of their nerves were frayed.

When he starts to talk to her, to try and apologize, she cuts him off, wanting to be the first one to talk. "No, babe," she says, "I am the one who should be saying sorry. I should have heard you out before I reacted the way I did and got mad. I guess I still have some trust issues and insecurities to work on myself. I'm realizing I need to trust you a little more, and maybe stress a little less about us."

It's in that moment that they both realize the other person has been upset about things they themselves weren't; while Demi has been stressing about trust and honesty, and about Adam keeping things a secret from her, Adam has been worried about her reacting badly to this jewelry heist and being mad at him for wanting to commit a bigger robbery, something so much more than gas and go's and $500 shopping sprees. Suddenly, all the tension that's been growing is gone, and things are as they always are between them again, hot, passionate, sexy, intense. Adam steps towards her as she leans in, and then they are all over each other, hands gripping one another tightly, pulling their bodies closer.

Adam's lips are cooler than hers from having been outside for a while, and Demi can taste the contrast of the beer on his breath verses the wine still lingering on hers. "You know," she moans between kisses, "all that beer from the mini fridge is going to cost us a fortune. It's a good thing we're just a modern-day version of Bonnie and Clyde, rich and always ready to rob from the richer." He half laughs at this, and half moans into her mouth, so turned on by what she's said that his already hard cock throbs in his jeans. The thrill of being involved in all of this with her gives him a rush he's never experienced before in his life, and he loves that she loves it too.

He can't help himself any longer; he needs to have her, right here, right now. His hands grab at the hem of her shirt, pulling on it, tugging it up over her head along with her bra and exposing her from the waist up on the balcony in the dark yellow lights of the city before them. Demi shivers, both from the cold air and from the sexual fire that's traveling through her veins, and she moans out loud. She reaches down and runs her fingers through his hair, as he begins to kiss along her neck and collar bone and makes his way down towards her breasts.

Her nipples are rock hard in the cool night breeze, and they grow even harder as she feels his tongue snake its way across one, flicking it lightly, covering it in spit and making her shudder. Demi moans and leans back against the patio door, the glass even colder against her skin, and she lets herself relax, allowing him to do as he pleases with her. One hand makes its way up her body, trailing along her smooth stomach, loving the softness of her skin under his fingers, until he reaches the gentle curve of her breast. He cups it firmly for a moment, and then slowly tweaks and pinches at her nipple until she arches herself against him, begging for more.

His other hand moves down the length of her body, along her curves, once more teasing the taunt skin of her smooth belly. He reaches the belt buckle of her pants and undoes them in one smooth motion, and then he grabs her pants and panties by the waist line and tugs them down to her ankles, leaving her naked and open to the cool air and the city before them. He hears her moan and feels her body shake against him, and he isn't sure whether that's from the chill or from what he's doing to her, but it only encourages him to continue.

Adam gently bites on the nipple that's in his mouth, causing her to moan louder, and he pinches the other one harder at the same time. He uses his leg to force her knees apart, letting the cold air reach her everywhere, causing goosebumps to form all over her skin, making her shiver.

Then ever so slowly he begins to kiss and lick and tease his way down her body, trailing his tongue along the bottom curve of her breast where she's most sensitive, turning her on even more. Her pussy throbs in anticipation for him. Her fingers are wrapped up in his hair, pushing on him and pulling him back, not sure whether she wants him to continue, or stop and take this inside, but her being so horny from his teasing and feeling very adventurous from the wine, she doesn't make him stop.

Demi stares out over the city lights in front of her as Adam slowly drops to his knees, using his hands to spread her legs open a little further. Her smell is intoxicating, and he can't wait to bury his face against her and taste her cum all over him. He uses his fingers to spread her lips open, and then leans forwards and begins to gently lick her clit, and she shudders once more, trying to stifle a moan from any nearby balcony mates. He reaches up and slides two fingers inside her, fucking her slowly, while still tonguing her softly, knowing just what she likes, rubbing her g-spot while he slowly sucks and licks on her little clit.

It's getting harder for her to keep quiet now, and she tries to use her hands to push Adam's head away from her as her moans get louder, wanting to take this inside now, but he won't stop, and instead only licks her faster, curling his fingers up inside of her as he slides them in and out, bringing her closer and closer to an orgasm. She tries to stop him one more time, but her hands feel weak, and she doesn't really want him to stop anyway, and ends up curling her fingers through his hair and pulling his face closer into her, throwing her head back against the patio door, pushing her hips upwards into him, letting herself go with it.

Adam can feel her getting closer now, and he grabs her thigh with his free hand and pushes it up over his shoulder, opening her to him completely. She moans louder now, no longer caring if anyone hears her, and gives herself up to him, letting him take her. He continues to lick her hard, little nub gently but faster now, rubbing his lips over it and sometimes pulling it lightly between them. His fingers never stop their assault on her dripping pussy, sliding in and out easily with how wet she is, her juices dripping down his hand, and he knows all the sweet spots inside her to rub and push her over the edge.

Demi can feel herself getting closer and closer; she's going to cum, right out here in the open night air. She moans as much to him, gripping his hair tightly in her hands, pulling his face into her. He feels her legs shudders around him; her body shakes, and she cries out as her orgasm begins to build.

Her silky pussy walls tighten around his fingers, and so do her thighs and the fingers in his hair as her orgasm overtakes her. He hears her moan his name aloud, and his already throbbing hard cock twitches in his jeans. His tongue moves down to her wet little hole, sucking on her and licking up all her juices, pulling her lips between his, not missing a single spot. He twists and swirls his tongue deep inside her, as far as he can go, feeling her still tightening and clenching as she slowly comes down from her high, licking up every drop of her cum.

Adam wastes no time now. He wants to be inside her, desperately, buried in her tight little pussy. He's been wanting to bang her since this afternoon, basically not more than a few hours after the last time they'd had sex, and the orgasm he'd given her in the car while driving, and then the heated fight they'd had, topped with this hot oral sex on the balcony, is enough to drive him over the edge, and almost make him want to cum in his pants, right now. Demi does something to him that he doesn't quite understand, she turns him on constantly, from her body and her over all sex appeal, right down to the way she laughs, the way she smells, the way her skin feels, to the way her mind works. She makes him feel like he is in high school again, hot and horny and always so desperate to be with her, and he doesn't mind one bit, except when he can't be with her when he wants.

He quickly stands up and grabs her by the waist and picks her up, pulling her into him, her naked body rubbing against his clothes, the contrast very erotic. He kisses her deeply, letting her taste herself on his tongue and his lips, and she moans into his mouth, loving it. He uses his foot to slide the balcony door open, and he carries her back inside the hotel room as she shuts the door behind them when they go through. He walks them right to the bathroom and sets her down on the vanity while he begins to strip off his clothes in front of her.

"Good," she says with a chuckle, watching him, "I won't be the only one naked anymore." He winks at her. "No, you love it. It makes you feel helpless and submissive to me, and that turns you on." The frankness in his voice, and the way he looks at her, makes her stomach flip flop, and the counter underneath her becomes slippery from her despite her having already had an orgasm outside. He sees the slight change in her body; the way she grips the counter a bit tighter, the way she flushes slightly, the way her breath catches in her throat, and he steps in to her and grabs her and pulls her into him, wrapping her legs around him, kissing her deeply while his cock presses up against her most sensitive area.

She moans into his mouth, and he can't take the teasing or the wait anymore, he needs to have her. Now. He pulls away from her and gets into the jacuzzi, turning the water on warm and putting the plug in, letting the water fill the tub. She gets in the tub behind him, and when he stands and turns around, she is sitting along the floor on the tub naked, awaiting the water to rise, eye level with his penis.

Demi licks her lips seductively, making eye contact with him, and he leans forward, gripping the side of the tub with one hand to steady himself. She reaches up, taking the base of his rock-hard member in one soft hand, lightly stroking him, from the base to the head, as he moans above her at her first gentle touch. She grips him with a little more strength and begins to jerk him off, an inch from her mouth, looking at him with porn star eyes and driving him crazy.

He moans louder and thrusts his hips towards her face, and she opens her mouth eagerly, sliding her soft wet tongue along the head of his cock and then twirling it around the shaft as she makes her way down. She times her licks slowly along with her strokes, rubbing him with her lips along the soft sensitive head as well as her tongue and hand, up and down, covering him in spit and driving him wild.

Adam can't take anymore; he's about to blow in her mouth, and that isn't where he wants to cum tonight. He pulls away and kneels in the jacuzzi in front of her, knees between hers, forcing her legs apart. Leaning down with his body against hers he slides them up along the back of the tub, water around their legs now, and rubs the head of his cock along her wet slit as he kisses her again, lips all over each other.

Demi moans and runs her hands along his back, pulling him into her, as his cock parts her wetness and slowly slides inside her tight hole. Adam moans into her neck and shoulder, his teeth grazing her skin, gripping her tightly in his hands as he begins to pound her into the side of the tub, her nails digging into his back, the water rising around them. Fucking her roughly until they both cry out in orgasm, clinging to each other tightly, holding each other close.

Chapter Five

When Demi opens her eyes the next morning, the sunlight streaming through the window almost blinds her. It feels far too early for a mid-day bright white sun. The pounding in her head is relentless; the cheap wine hangover she is feeling seems like there is a rock concert playing full blast somewhere, and all she's getting is the booming bass, thumping and echoing through her head. The scratchy hotel sheets are clinging to her, wrapped around her aching, sweaty body, and she stretches lazily in the bed, pointing her toes and reaching her arms high above her, fingers grazing the headboard, letting out a big, lazy, morning yawn.

The bed shifts beside her, and she hears Adam moan as he slowly joins her in the real world. By the low, almost painful sound of it though, he is probably far worse off than she is right now, having had way more to drink than she did. A quick glance around the hotel room tells her everything that she needs to know to fill in the blanks that alcohol took from her last night; there are bottles strewn all over the room, the counters, and leading back to the bathroom. Snack packages are all over the counters too, as well as the bedside tables, and their clothes are all thrown around the room, her bra hanging off the back of a chair, his pants tossed in the corner. There are towels half out of the bathroom, and the jacuzzi is still filled with cold, soapy water, and beer bottles surround the tub. This morning, or whatever time this is, is not going to be good to them.

Adam rolls over next to her and drapes his arm around her middle, pulling her closer into him, pressing himself up against her. She feels his erection poke her in the side of her thigh, and she realizes they are both naked under the white sheets. "Good morning," he whispers to her groggily, kissing along her collar bone and her neck, making her shiver. "Well, good morning to you too handsome, although I think it's probably closer to lunch time." Demi replies with a laugh, and rolls over into him, wrapping her arms around him and kissing him back gently.

The mood between them is a lot lighter and happier now, since they've gotten over their feelings and insecurities last night and smoothed everything out amongst one another again. Things are almost normal, well, if there is such a thing as normal in their relationship. After a few shared kisses they slowly drag themselves out of bed, and they make their way into the shower to clean and freshen up before they start the day. Now that things are a little more relaxed, Demi is willing to hear Adam out and listen to his plan and see where things may lead them.

Demi climbs in the shower first, stripping slowly and then just standing there under the stream of hot water for a few minutes, feeling lazy, letting it warm her right through to the bone. Adam gets in the shower behind her and just holds her, wrapping his arms around her waist, letting the water run over them both, enjoying one another's company, and just being in the moment. She turns around slowly, and lets the water run through her hair, and he takes the shampoo from the side and puts some in the palm of his hands and begins to lather her hair up for her. It isn't a sexual act, it's far more sensual, intimate, and Demi all but melts from the feeling of his fingers running along her scalp and through her hair, pampering her, before he moves onto the soap, lathering his hands again and running them all over her body, feeling her soapy body everywhere under his hands.

Afterwards, she stands still for a few moments and lets the water run through her hair, and down her body, slowly rinsing herself off, letting the hot water wake her up. When she feels clean she slides to the side and lets Adam move past her under the spray of water, and then she slides to the back of the shower, thinking about getting out. But he's suddenly behind her, his arm around her waist again, pulling her into him, his hard cock pressing against her slippery ass. "Watching that soapy water run down your body turns me on so much," he said, using his free hand to grip his cock at the base, and sliding it up and down her wet slit.

Moaning loudly, she places her hands on the shower wall in front of her and raises one of her legs up onto the side of the tub, stepping on the ledge, spreading herself open to him. Adam still has his cock in his hand and he wastes no time pressing the head of it up against her tight hole, and he slides inside of her in one smooth motion. Demi moans loudly, and he pushes them up against the cool wall, her nipples rock hard against the cold tile, as he starts to pound into her. His cock slips in and out of her easily as she's so wet, the heat of the shower and the hair washing, as well as only being half awake, being wonderful foreplay.

He runs his hands up her slender, tight body, along her stomach and over her chest, caressing her boobs and tweaking on her nipples as he passes over them, making them even harder. She presses herself back into him, moving her hips against his with every thrust. He knows he isn't going to last long, and he picks up speed while moving his hand back down her body. His fingers find her hard-little clit between her wet folds and she cries out and presses herself against him as he starts to rub her gently, touching all her sweet spots as he fucks her, pulling her in close, bringing her to orgasm with him.

They cum together up against the wall, breathing heavily and moaning softly, Adam all but holding her up against him as the water flows around them, her knees and body feeling weak, clinging to him.

Shortly afterwards they are both dressed, and they've each done a quick once over tidy of the hotel room, removing all the garbage, food wrappers and all the cans and bottles from the large amount of alcohol they had both consumed the night before, and tossed all their dirty clothes in a pile. Once Demi thinks the place is clean enough for room service to come in, which Adam thinks is hilariously ridiculous, but still super cute of her, they grab their jackets, keys, purse and wallet and head out on a walk to a nearby breakfast place, so they can talk a little more, and get some coffee into them to wake up a bit and fill their bellies.

It's a chillier day, but not too cold, and the walk is refreshing as they make their way down the street. They don't talk much, but they do hold hands, just enjoying each other's company now that things are happier between them again. They arrive at the restaurant a few minutes later, and they decide on a booth near the back, away from other diners and most of the rest of the place, so that they can have a little privacy and talk in quiet, so Adam can tell her his plans.

After the waitress has come and gone, taking their orders of bacon, eggs, home fries, toast, and lots and lots of coffee, Adam begins to open up to her and discuss the plan that he's begun to hatch. Despite their make up last night, and how easy things seem between them this late morning wake up, he's still a bit nervous to talk to her about it and finds himself fidgeting with his coffee cup while he talks, worried that things are going to go south between them again.

"I think it would be the perfect crime, because it's a double jeopardy, and won't even be reported or handled by police in the traditional sense. And it's huge. HUGE. It's not like anything we've been involved with before, which makes it all that much more exciting, and thrilling, and worth it." Demi doesn't say much while he talks; she simply holds her coffee mug between her hands, warming herself, sipping on it occasionally, and listens to what he has to say.

"A friend of mine has been talking about robbing his ex-boss for a long time. He's got a personal grudge against the guy, for work related reasons, and he's been casing and researching this place for months now. He's even got blueprints and photos of the house and of the safes and everything. He knows the guys schedule, along with his wife's, and when he's going to be gone away on holidays. He just doesn't have the guts to go through with it. And the guy my buddy wants to rob? He's a jewelry store owner. About a year ago, he claimed a robbery, a massive one that left him with nothing, and reported every damn thing stolen, including a ton of cash. Except he was never robbed at all. He stole from himself, and then banked in on the insurance money too. So technically, the crime has already been committed.

My buddy knows all this because he was the grounds keeper there for a long time and saw a couple safes move into the place a little while beforehand, and some shady stuff went on around there at the time of the robbery, including all the staff being fired and paid off with no notice.

Joe started keeping an eye on the place, even going as far as to peek in the windows at night and confirmed all his thoughts about the jewelry. The guy is just sitting on it for now, millions in cash and jewels, waiting for enough time to pass. Joe knows where to dump the jewelry and everything, and besides, there's a lot of cash at stake too, but like I said, he just doesn't have the guts. We do. And I think it would be incredibly exciting, and it's something I can't stop thinking about doing, and doing with you. I think it's worth it. What do you think?"

The food arrives just as Adam finishes talking, and they both fall silent for a few minutes, preparing their late breakfasts and beginning to eat, both thinking over what he's just told them. Adam is more concerned about her reaction than anything. He is still a little uncertain how she is going to take all of this, if she will want to go forward with him, or not, and what she's thinking of him right now. His head is a mess, and he hates the anxiety that he gets when he thinks about the unknown with her. He loves her so much, but sometimes he feels like he's walking on eggshells, and he doesn't even know whose fault that really is, or how to fix it.

Demi chews slowly, savoring her food, Adams plans jumping all over the place inside of her head, racing a mile ahead of her. She can see all the sides to it now, of course, with a clear sober mind, and having been willing to hear him out. Really, this is just another step up from the path that they are already traveling down, and one that she had agreed to as well. She knows she cannot fault him for coming up with this plan. This had all started from her, and was fed by the excitement it caused, the thrill of it, the sexual energy it gave them, and nothing else.

Money was not an issue for them, at least not right now. Between Adam's ransom money, and the funds she had drawn from her accounts before they left, they have money stashed everywhere, and aren't concerned about the dollar signs. However, she knows that money isn't going to last forever, and it wouldn't hurt to replenish their stash. Plus, the excitement that would come from robbing someone else's personal house, and their already stolen jewelry and stacks of money… The thought gives her a thrill she hasn't felt yet, and her body shudders like she's caught a cold.

She realizes that her mind has begun to wander when she finds herself thinking about what it would be like to fuck him on a fancy hotel bed surrounded by stolen jewels, and stacks of stolen cash. Her vagina grows wet, and she crosses her legs under the table, pressing her thighs together and putting pressure on herself. If thinking about it makes her this hot, then they definitely need to go through with it. She nods slowly, looking him in the eye, and tells him that she's game, and asks him what their next move is.

Chapter Six

Adam and Demi spend the next few days driving from place to place, state by state, towards the city the jeweler lives in. They trade off driving, but they don't drive too late into the nights this time, instead getting caught up on some rest and down time together at roadside hotels, as they aren't in much of a rush to get there. The next time the jeweler is scheduled to leave again with his wife on holidays is two weeks from now, so they have lots of time to arrive in his city, get settled at a hotel and prepare for real.

They talk a lot about the plan in general, without getting too specific until they've really had a chance to sit down and go over everything, not wanting to get stuck on something that might not be feasible. They know they'll need to spend some time gathering supplies, doing some research online, they'll have to case the place out, and get familiar with it outside of the photographs. They'll have to go over those in great detail too, the photographs and the blueprints of the house, and Adam is going to have to make sure he knows what he's doing with the safes, too. There are still a lot of details that need to be worked out, if this is all going to go over smoothly.

When they aren't talking about the upcoming heist, they are talking about themselves, and opening up to each other. As things are still new between them, and developing rather unconventionally, they are still learning as they go, seeing where they fit. Discovering one another's hopes, dreams, needs, fears, pasts, wants. Finding out who the other person is, inside and out, and falling more in love with each other as they go.

Since they are making good time, even without driving at night, and not being in a rush to get there, the pair end up taking an entire day off the road and just sightsee around a city, and act like a couple of complete tourists. They buy a local map and take a cab and check out all the places that seem interesting. They each have their own likes, and dislikes, and this ends up being a fun and enjoyable way to get to know each other a little more too. Everything about their relationship has been a whirlwind from the start, and they've never really dated either, just sort of jumped in with both feet and took a chance. The chemistry between them is unbelievable though, and they're a couple of horny teenagers when they are together; unsustainable, they can never get enough.

Feelings have developed between them fast though, despite how they started, and all the other strikes against them. Demi chalks that up to being in close quarters all the time, right from the beginning, paired with their wild sexual attraction for each other and the events that brought them together, but Adam isn't so sure. She drives him crazy, in almost every sense of the word, not just in a sexual way, and he has been falling in love with her something bad right from the start. They have both dropped the L word a few times, but Adam thinks this is something far more than the starting of love. He already knows he's head over heels for her, and can't imagine life without her anymore, or what he would be doing with himself right now if the events of his life hadn't lead him to kidnapping her that night with Brandon. He can't see his future without her in it.

Adam also has a hard time believing they are where they are, together as a couple, doing what they're doing together right now, robbing and stealing and planning this big heist. Once he reconnected with her in the park after Brandon had let her go, he would have done absolutely anything to stay in her life. Been whatever she wanted. Gone wherever she pleased. Lived whatever kind of life she chose. But it rocked his whole world that in the end, it was her that had followed him on this crazy adventure, packed up all the important things she owned, and emptied her accounts, got in the car with him, and drove off into the unknown.

This adventure that was unfolding in front of them was unlike anything he had ever experienced in his life, and he was ever so grateful it was with Demi. He would have followed her to the ends of the earth, but it meant so much more that she was following him; giving her ideas and input as they went along, sure, but in the end, it had been his idea to just hit the road, and then keep on with what they were doing, and she was clearly coming along for the whole ride. He had no idea what the future would bring. For all he knew, they could be arrested or go to jail at any point for some of the crazy things they'd done so far. But it was worth it. Every single, wild moment with her had been worth it, and he wouldn't change a thing.

Breaking himself out of his thoughts, he reaches across the seat towards her as he drives and takes her hand in his own. Adam takes a glance over at her and she looks at him and smiles, her eyes smiling too, and squeezes his hand back, settling herself into the seat. Nope, he thinks again to himself, he wouldn't change a single moment.

Chapter Seven

After a few more days of traveling through the country side, checking things off their sightseeing list, and having lots and lots of roadside sex and kinky hotel sex, the pair end up in Colorado just before lunch, the city where the jeweler and his wife live. They drive around for a little while, checking out the area, and then they settle on a smaller, inconspicuous hotel towards the outskirts of the city that takes cash and doesn't require any identification. Adam has gotten into the habit of making sure they don't ever leave much of a trail behind them, if at all, just in case.

Demi is insistent that she have some time to shower, change into fresh clothes and get herself settled again, and even though Adam is antsy to do something more productive now that they're here, he agrees. He knows that nothing about this heist can be sloppy or rushed, and that they must be smart about every move, and every single detail. A little bit of time to freshen up and recharge their batteries would do them both some good after all this time on the road. And once they're in the room, and he lays down on the bed for a moment while she unpacks a bit and gets ready for a shower, it isn't long before he's snoring away on top of the bedsheets, having himself a little afternoon catnap, all thoughts of being productive long behind him for a while.

A few hours later, once they've both had a chance to get rested and refreshed, changed and showered, they leave the hotel and walk down the street a way, exploring the area close to them, and they find a small diner to eat a late lunch / early supper at. With all the driving and weird hours that they've been keeping lately, their schedules are so messed up, and it's rare that they sleep or eat at the appropriate times.

They go inside and settle themselves into a booth near the back and wait until the waitress has come and gone with their drink and food orders before they start talking business. Adam has been doing a lot of thinking while they've been driving, and when Demi was the one behind the wheel, he had also been doing research from his laptop and the ghost phone he'd acquired, and only using the WIFI hot spots they passed. He had gotten a hold of all the photographs and blueprints that they needed, and even more information on the couple they were robbing, information on the safes, the jewels, and gathered more of a plan in general, and he was eager to finally share all of that with her in one big go, and make a good, solid plan of action together.

"I figure we will start by driving past the place and through the area, getting comfortable with the house, streets and neighborhood in general." He starts. "We should also spend some time in the hotel room going over all the information I've gotten together, like the pictures and blueprints and even some of the history on the place, and of the couple themselves. We never know what might come in handy."

The waitress comes back at that point with their drinks and some of the condiments for their dinner, and Adam pauses, waiting for her to leave. Demi sips her drink slowly, thinking over everything he's said to her so far as he goes on.

"I think that we should walk by the place on foot a couple times, during the day once for sure and at night twice, maybe even sneak onto the property once as well and really scope the place out if we can. My buddy has given me some very detailed property descriptions, and we should be able to hop over a broken part of the fence where a tree has grown into it in the backyard. I'll show you the photos at the hotel. I need to go over the safes, and some other fine details too, so while I'm doing that, you can go over all the pictures and paperwork details that you do so well, and the history of everything. And help me fine tune the plans and the details as we put it all together."

As she's thinking about everything and what to say next, their food arrives, and they spend a few moments in silence as they prepare their plates and start to eat. Adam is starving, and begins to eat right away, but Demi is distracted though, pushing her food around on her plate. It's not really what he's said that's distracted her, but rather it's how this is all making her feel.

She still doesn't understand it, but everything about their illegal activities turns her on almost as much as he does. From that very first gas and go that she had performed accidentally, and then found herself sopping wet after while they'd fucked on the side of the road, she knew that this was some weird fetish for her. One that must stem from her rich have everything upbringing, or need for attention, or something. Especially considering here she was again, panties soaked at the diner booth, as she pushes her food around on her plate, trying to force herself to concentrate on the plans he's told her, and not how badly she just wants to crawl under the table and do naughty things to him, right here in front of everyone.

Adam can sense something is up with her though. He has been watching her as he's been telling her the plans so far, still a little bit antsy about how everything was going to work out, but about part way through what he'd been saying, he'd seen Demi's eyes get that lost, glossy look that she gets when she's horny, or thinking about something that turns her on, and he can't help but question to himself what she's actually thinking about, or if it's just the heist talk itself that's doing it for her right now.

He watches her body language for a few more minutes as she's thinking to herself. The way she's just pushing her food around on her plate, not really eating even though she should have a good appetite by now, and the way she's shifting in her seat, pressing her legs together and crossing and uncrossing them constantly like she's uncomfortable even though she should be plenty comfortable on that cushion seat that she's sitting on, confirms what he's been thinking. She's getting turned on in the middle of this diner surrounded by people while they talk quietly about their planned robbery. Her kinky side still amazes him and turns him on like crazy too.

Adam leans in closer to her, laying his arms on the table and taking her free hand in his, breaking her train of thought, and she looks up at him to see him smiling wickedly at her. Demi feels herself blush deep red in embarrassment, suddenly knowing that he knows what she's been thinking about. He was talking very softly before, as to not be overheard, but now he all but whispers to her. "Is all this talk turning you on? Are you horny right now, thinking about this heist we're going to do??"

If Demi thought she was blushing before, she is even more so now, turning another shade darker, and she looks away from him, down at her plate. Then she nods, biting her bottom lip, suddenly feeling extremely submissive to him in this busy public place. "Of course, you are, you bad girl," he says with a smirk, and she feels it all the way through her body, her pussy throbbing at the sound of his voice. "Maybe I'll have to take you back to the hotel and show you how much I love what a bad girl you are," he says, but his voice lingers there, and Demi's eyes jolt up as she realizes he has something more to say, wondering what else he's got up his sleeve for her.

"But I think before we do that we're going to need to make a stop at a sex shop first. I don't think I'm properly prepared to show you everything that I'm thinking about right now." Demi's entire body trembles at the thought, and she knows her underwear are all but drenched. She shifts in her seat again and starts to eat her dinner, eager for them to finish up and leave, excited and nervous for what he was planning to do to her later that night.

Chapter Eight

Demi's entire body is trembling, but she doesn't know if it's from the chill of the cool air on her naked body, or if it's from the excitement, and the unknown, of what lies ahead for her tonight. She's feeling nervous too, although only a little bit, as she trusts Adam, and she's also feeling anxious for things to start. The waiting, and anticipation, is driving her absolutely crazy, and adding to the way she's feeling. And she's sure that's part of his plans for the night. Teasing her and holding her off is only the beginning of what he's got in store for her.

She is currently tied with her limbs out to the sides, spread eagle and face down, on the hotel bed. Adam has strung ropes around underneath the mattress and then up the sides so that her arms and legs are all tied down to the edges, and she's unable to move. She is also blindfolded, but "only for now" he'd said to her when he put it on. She already knew the room was dark, he'd lit candles and turned off all the lights before he blindfolded her, and then he told her he was going into the bathroom for a few minutes to prepare for their night, and that she'd have no choice but to wait for her punishment. And he wasn't kidding about making her wait for it; it has been quite some time now and she's feeling restless, and very helpless, hoping he will come back out for her at any second, and dole out whatever punishment he's got in mind.

Every single sound she hears, movement from other rooms, noise from the city outside their windows, people's voices in the hallway, it all makes her jump, feeling on pins and needles, so when she finally does hear him come up beside her on the bed, she almost cries out, startled. He doesn't make a sound, he just sits on the bed beside her, and she feels the mattress shift under her with his weight added to it. Then, she feels his fingers trail up her back, ever so lightly and gently, almost tickling her, and everything inside of her feels like it sets on fire all at once.

She's helpless under his light caresses that move up her back, along her shoulder blades, and then slowly travel back down her spine, making her moan out loud. Softly, the tips of his fingers trail along the cheeks of her ass, then down the back of one of her sensitive thighs, again teasing her and almost tickling her at the same time, and she bites her bottom lip to keep herself from crying out. His fingers slide over to her other thigh and slowly make their way back up that one now, and she tries to shift her hips in her restraints, desperately hoping that he'll make his way towards the aching wetness between her legs that's desperate for him.

Instead, she feels them lightly brush the underside of the curve of where her thigh meets her bum, the sensitive area he's rubbing and his soft caress making her shudder and moan once more. His fingers move up the curve of her ass again, and then he pulls his hand away, and she's left longing for him, aching for him, and again tries to pull against her restraints, raising her hips upwards, longing for his touch.

Smack! Adam's flat palm comes down hard on her unsuspecting ass cheek, making her flinch, and this time she does cry out, although not quite in the same way she had wanted to just a moment before. And as if it's possible, her pussy throbs and gets even more wet, feeling like she's starting to soak the bed sheets underneath her. "I'd be quiet if I were you," he says to her in a hoarse whisper, leaning down close to the side of her face, "Or I'll have to gag you next." She bites her bottom lip again, turning her head away and stifling any more sounds she wants to make right now, loving the sexual authority he has over her, loving being helpless to him.

She feels his hand on her again, softly this time, and his fingertips make their way gently over the red spot on her ass that his spanking left, caressing where it's sore and sensitive. Slowly, his hand moves again over the slope of the top of her cheeks and down to her lower back; she breaks out in goosebumps as he runs his fingers up the length of her spine again, ever so softly, almost tickling her once more. He lightly glides his fingers through her hair at the base of her spine, causing her to shudder again and moan under her breath, and then he moves his hand upwards towards the top of her head, and he grabs a handful of her hair unexpectedly, tightly in his hand, and pulls her head back forcefully, her ear close to his waiting mouth, his breath hot on her skin.

"I told you I was going to punish you earlier, remember that. But don't think for a second that it's just from earlier either." He straddles her, still pulling on her hair, and his free hand roams her body as she's pulled tight against her restraints. Her pussy throbs in anticipation of what's to come, with his hands all over her, helpless to him, and her mind begins to race all over the map, wondering what he's talking about. "I believe there is still that little incident at the farm house where you tried to run away from me and made me chase you, naked and all, that I've yet to properly punish you for."

Demi feels her breath catch in her throat, remembering all too well now exactly what he's talking about, the night she tried to escape from the farm house, and her kidnappers. The night she tried to use him sexually. Her face flushes, and she's grateful she's still blindfolded, so she doesn't have to see him right now.

Adam lets go of her hair, letting her head drop back down to the mattress, and he slides back off her slender body and delivers another hard smack to her cheek, making her ass tingle and causing her to bite her lip once more to keep from crying out. This spank is followed by a second, and then a third. Not hard enough to really hurt her, but hard enough to make her tingle and moan, and to remind her that right now, here in this hotel room, in this moment, he's the boss and in control of her, and she's being punished.

Demi knows her butt is probably a nice shade of red by now, and she is starting to really get into it, turned on beyond belief. She is so wet, the bed sheets beneath her are beginning to feel wet against her skin as well. And she's starting to match his spankings, raising her hips a little bit higher against her restraints every time, aching for more.

Adam laughs a little at her eagerness, and calls her a bad little girl again, loving the sounds that she's making beneath him, loving the way she's responding to his touch. Instead of spanking her again, this time he rubs his hands along her red behind gently when she thrusts her hips up to meet him. She's warm to the touch, and slithering all over the bed underneath his fingertips, feeling hypersensitive, wanting more and wanting him to stop all at the same time.

Adam slides his hands up her body, along the length of her sides, along her arms, almost laying himself down on the bed beside her. He runs his hands through her hair again, pulling her head to the side, and kisses her neck softly, his touch so gentle now, making her moan. He keeps touching her everywhere, teasing her, palms and fingertips caressing and massaging her blind, helpless body, while he lightly licks and kisses along her neck and collar bone and shoulder area, driving her nuts.

If she thought she was wet before, she is absolutely soaking now, her silky folds between her legs throbbing and aching for the touch he's giving the rest of her body but denying where she wants it most. She's pulling against her restraints now, desperate for him, needing more. She can't help herself anymore, it's all too much for her, and a small, whispered "please" passes her lips, begging him before she can help herself.

Instantly, she feels Adam pull away from her on the bed, his hands and mouth no longer near her, and she knows she should have stayed quiet. Her body aches for him, and she's only making it worse. He moves closer to her ear again, his breath hot and teasing on her skin once more. "Do you need another reminder of who's boss again? Because I will gladly gag you." His tongue snakes out between his lips and licks along the length of her ear lobe and down her neck, and her body shudders again. She stays quiet, biting her lip.

Adam sits up and straddles her naked body again, his hard cock pressed up against her back. He continues his assault on her body with his hands and fingers and lips and tongue, teasing her everywhere, driving her crazy. She is not the only one being teased right now though, he is solid as a rock and dripping precum all over her, and he'd love to lean back and slide the head of his cock in her and take her in one smooth motion. But he keeps going, slowly, ever so slowly kissing and touching and teasing, working his way down her body, taking his time and making it last.

Demi is on fire. Every part of her is sensitive, screaming, throbbing, desperate. She has her face all but buried in the mattress to stifle her moans and cries. Her nipples are hard and stiff against the bed beneath her, rubbing against the fabric roughly, driving her crazy every time she shifts around. Her pussy feels like it's swollen, it's so sensitive and wet and aching. Her body is trembling and pulling against her restraints. She just wants to feel him part her lips and slide inside of her. She just wants him to make her cum.

His hands are still on her body, everywhere, but finally they begin to make their way down along her ass cheeks again, and across the back of her hips and thighs. She almost cries out again and begs for him to fuck her, she's so sensitive and horny, needy and desperate, but she bites her lip and pushes her face back into the mattress beneath her, keeping quiet and remembering his rule, letting him have his way with her, letting him take her when he will.

Adam grabs her thighs and presses his thumbs into the inner upper part of them, and parts her sensitive area slowly, opening her up to him, making her squirm even more as he exposes her. He massages the back of her legs softly, letting her relax, sliding his firm palms up and down the back and insides of her thighs, so sensitive and wet from her juice. His thumbs slide up more still, until they brush against the soft spot where her legs meet the inside of her lips, and she moans out loud, even with her face buried. He laughs softly and runs his thumbs gently from there up towards her ass and back down again, causing her to pull against her restraints and cry out again.

Demi isn't being quiet anymore, but he isn't going to be able to take much more of this either. He leans forward, and the head of his cock brushes against her wet slit, making her gasp, just touching her gently before he pulls away, and her hips instantly arch back against him, eager to have him fill her. He grabs the base of his cock in his hands and rubs her with the head of it again, sliding it up and down her wet lips, with a little firmer pressure this time, then pulling away again when she thrusts back to meet him.

She groans in frustration, and he gives in suddenly, sliding into her sopping hole and bottoming out in her in one smooth thrust. Her groan turns into a loud moan of pleasure as he pulls out again, almost all the way, before filling her again, roughly, feeling her tight walls clench around him. He leans down and pulls her tied body into his, his chest sweaty against her back, taking her and fucking her hard, owning her, his fingers gripping her tightly as he slides his cock in and out of her.

It's not going to take her long to cum after he's teased her for so long, and he knows that, however he also knows he's going to cum right there with her, so horny and aching for her too. He picks up his speed, hammering into her, her slippery pussy like velvet around his hard cock as he pounds her. He licks along the back of her ear, kissing her neck, feeling her body shudder beneath him as she gets closer and closer to cumming. Demi feels his hand slide down and pinch one of her nipples hard, and then slides lower, under her stomach, and his fingers part her folds and rub her clit hard as he takes her roughly from behind.

Demi feels herself being pushed over the edge, helplessly taken like this, at his mercy, his hands and mouth all over her, his hard cock buried into her. She cries out and arches back into him, pulling against her restraints, feeling them bite into her skin, not caring at all, giving in to her orgasm. Adam growls in her ear, thrusting hard against her, forcing her down into the mattress, cumming deep inside her as she moans and cums all over his pulsing cock, her pussy milking him.

Afterwards, with both of them breathing heavy, Demi relaxes into the mattress, no longer straining on her limbs, and feels Adam's weight come down half on her and half on the bed beside her. He rips the blindfold off, kissing her deeply, and pulls her body tightly against his, still tied to the bed.

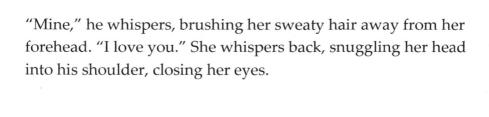

"Mine," he whispers, brushing her sweaty hair away from her forehead. "I love you." She whispers back, snuggling her head into his shoulder, closing her eyes.

Chapter Nine

The next few days go by in a fast, productive blur as the pair are on the go constantly, getting ready for the heist. There is a bit of shopping for them to do to in order to gather everything they're going to need to be fully prepared, and Adam is very persistent that they be specific about how and where they do their shopping, even though the risk involved for them is very minimal. He insists they only purchase certain items at certain stores, they must go alone, and they never buy related items together. Just gathering up everything they need takes up a lot of time, a little more than Adam's planned for, but he's satisfied they are still covering all their tracks.

They still have lots of research and prep work to do as well. Demi spends some time going over the photographs, blueprints and house history that Adam has put together very thoroughly, while Adam perfects what he needs to do involving the safes, mostly making sure he's going to be able to open them alright, and in the amount of time that they'll have for him to do so. He spends a lot of time on the computer and on the ghost phone too, making sure that everything is lined up perfectly for them, finalizing every single last detail.

While all of this is going on, Adam finds himself reflecting on the fact that they've not only been sharing a lot of close quarters recently, but that most of their entire relationship has been them cooped up together; between the kidnapping, driving around the country for a few weeks and all that time in the car, and now this time spent together getting ready for the heist, held up in hotel rooms and scooping out places in the car. They have been together, and almost always alone together, mostly in a vehicle, since the very start of their relationship.

It definitely isn't conventional, he thinks to himself, but he wouldn't have changed it for anything. It's given him a real chance to get to know her, emotionally and intimately. They've had all the time in the world for talking, and they could talk to each other for hours and hours without getting tired of listening to the other or running out of stories to tell the other either.

But as much as Adam loves hearing her talk, and loves listening to her stories, they're always bittersweet stories for him. As he falls more and more in love with her, he aches more and more for her and everything terrible that she's ever been through, including what he and Brandon have done to her as well, even though it did lead him to her. It hurts him that he's another painful experience in her life, and he's determined to make up for that.

Demi's voice interrupts his thoughts, letting him know that she could use a break, and to get out of the hotel room for a while, to clear her head and stretch her legs, and he whole heartedly agrees with her. As they gather up a few things, Adam decides to take a drive past the house first before they go out for something to eat, and Demi laughs upon hearing this. "Seriously, are we going to do this again for the umpteenth time hun? I know you want this to go perfectly and all, but I think we could do this in our sleep by now."

Adam laughs along with her, but that doesn't stop him from still insisting that they take a drive by before stopping for dinner.

A short while later, they drive by the street, seeing the house from afar before making a few left turns in the subdivision and driving close by the actual house. Adam goes over the plan out loud again, even though at this point Demi has it memorized. "We'll come by the place in the evening twice, before we rob it. We should check it out in the dark, tonight, both here in the car and on foot, and then we will come back tomorrow night and actually get onto the property and make sure we can pull this off. And I know that may seem risky, but it's very secluded back behind the house, and I would rather a few small risks to make sure everything goes smoothly, then run in blinded and risk it all, for nothing anyway." Demi laughs again at his thoroughness, and how seriously he's taking this, but the thrill turns her on like crazy, and she knows he's right with all his rules and ideas.

Plus, that dominate, take charge side of him drives her wild. It was probably what attracted her to her kidnapper in the first place, besides his sexy body, and the tattoos she loves. She runs her hand up his leg, distracting him from his thoughts, bringing him onto the same level as she is. "We should go grab a bite to eat for dinner and take a break somewhere, before we have to come back here for this "night watch" later. Let's go do something together for fun." She says, and he agrees, pulling out of the subdivision and heading back towards the main drag of the city, so they can get some food to eat and plan for something afterwards.

Once they've stopped at a quick corner diner and enjoy a meal together, they leave the car parked there and take a walk down towards the river. Holding hands, Adam and Demi head upstream, making small talk, killing time and mostly just enjoying each other's company, taking a bit of a break from everything that's been going on. A little way up the river there is an open park area with benches and flower beds and some lovely spots to sit and watch the water roll by for a while, so they pick a cozy spot on a patch of grass and do just that.

It is quiet for a little while, as they cuddle together, just resting and thinking about everything that's happened, and everything that is still to come over the next few nights. Still holding hands, Demi runs her thumb up and down lightly along Adam's, as his foot nudges hers gently while they lay snuggled up quietly. Adam laughs suddenly, softly, and Demi looks at him questioningly, his laugh catching her off guard in the silence. "I was just thinking," he begins, "that we met under such crazy circumstances, and then everything afterwards has been so crazy as well, I wonder if that's how it was meant to be, or how it's supposed to be now. Pretty wild story to ever tell people though." Demi laughs at this and snuggles up closer to him. "Well, we're both a little crazy anyway," she replies, "so I think that's alright."

Adam pulls her in tighter, wrapping his arms around her, watching the water flow along slowly in front of them. "I love you," he says, kissing the top of her head, smelling the scent of hotel shampoo in her hair. "And I love you," she replies, closing her eyes and enjoying the moment. "Hey, don't you fall asleep on me," he says jokingly, nudging her. She opens her eyes and laughs. "I think it's a bit chilly out here for a nap. However, I wouldn't turn down a siesta at the hotel before we go back out tonight."

He agrees, and they slowly get up and start walking back to the diner where they've parked the car, and then back to the hotel, knowing a late evening nap would help them stay up most of the night watching the place, awake and alert, making sure everything is ready for their heist.

Chapter Ten

It is much later, and night has fallen when the pair return to the subdivision; they are all stocked up on snacks, coffee, drinks and goodies to keep them busy and occupied while they wait out the evening tucked away in the car. They drove around other areas of the city for a while too, checking out the sights and killing time until it got dark enough to stake the place out. Once the moon rises a little bit later, Adam turns the car back towards the house and they park a little way further down the street, the opposite side of where they were parked when they stopped to check the place out quickly the day before. Adam turns the car off, and everything grows quiet once the rumble of the engine dies, as they sit in anticipation of what's to come.

Adam is still determined for them to keep a low profile and make sure nothing they do seems sketchy or leaves a trail behind them. Not only are they parked on the other side of the house on the other street this time, but he's also tucked them in behind another car that seems to be parked for the night, and he's brought binoculars so that they can be that much further away and stay safe, while still keeping a close eye on the place.

They both take turns watching the house, and they pass the time shifting around in their seats, listening to music, talking about anything and everything and snacking. There is a tension between them though; it's sexual tension left over from earlier, not having taken the time to enjoy one another earlier in the day, not since their morning shower together, and as the time crawls by, and it feels like it's passing slower and slower, the tension between them grows and grows.

Adam is watching her shift around in the passenger seat, occasionally sipping at her coffee, and he knows it's not entirely from restlessness anymore that's got her wiggling around like that. And, being the kind of man that he is, he planned ahead for this exact thing, he even remembered to bring a few things to have fun with while they wait. As she shifts around in her seat again, Adam reaches out and brushes a strand of hair from her face, tucking it behind her ear, drawing her attention towards him. She smiles and lets out a small sigh, and he leans forward and kisses her gently, just brushing her lips with his own, and sparks fly.

His light touches always give her shivers, and she feels her body instantly react to his teasing kiss. She leans towards him, kissing him back harder, opening her mouth a little and running the tip of her tongue along his bottom lip, knowing what he likes. He growls a little under his breath and grabs her and pulls her upper body closer to his across the seats, kissing her back passionately for a moment. He feels her start to respond to his kissing, her tongue urgently rubbing against his, and he pulls away, leaving her hanging and disappointed, and wanting more.

Demi sighs and leans back in her seat, getting comfortable and taking a deep breath, looking out the window. She had been enjoying that, but she knows that they're here for an important reason, so they shouldn't really be getting distracted; even if she does love kissing him and touching him, and knows he feels the same.

She thinks about reaching for her coffee when suddenly he is leaning over her again, his breath hot against her skin; yet this time he doesn't touch her. Instead, he reaches around her and stretches his arm down the side of her seat and pulls the recliner for her seat, dropping her backwards and laying her out in front of him, startling her and almost taking her breath away.

Then she squeals and lets out a giggle, thinking to herself that if she had reached for her coffee she would have been wearing it now. Demi looks up as he is glancing down at her, and her stomach flip flops at the expression on his face. Adam leans down as if to kiss her, and then instead brushes his lips along the side of her neck as he leans across her a second time and reaches and rummages for something he has tucked behind her seat. She shivers in anticipation, wondering what he has in store for her now.

Adam sits up a bit, keeping what's in his hand hidden behind the seat still, and he kisses her again, deeply, pushing his tongue into her mouth and forcing her into the seat with his body. She relaxes under his touch, kissing him back eagerly, and feels one of his hands move up to her shoulder and slowly touch and trace along the skin of her neck and collar bone, ever so lightly, giving her goosebumps. As he continues to kiss her, his fingers trail down her arm, along the sensitive underside of her upper arm and along her elbow and then down to her wrist. That he takes in his hand, wrapping his fingers around her slender wrist bones, and begins to slowly pull her hand and arm away from her body and back behind the seat.

Without breaking the kiss, and keeping her pinned to her seat, he reaches for her other hand with his free hand, gripping that wrist gently, and now tugs both of her hands behind the seat, pinning her further. He breaks their kiss, pulling away slightly, and looking into her eyes with a smirk, not saying a word to her, he begins to tie her wrists together behind the seat, keeping her stuck in her seat.

The look in his eyes, one of total dominance and control, of lust and need, paired with suddenly being laid out and tied to her seat, almost helpless at his mercy, makes her stomach flip flop once more and her pussy grow wet with excitement. She can't help but let out a moan in anticipation, not having expected this, and not knowing where he's going with it.

Adam sits back a bit in his own seat and takes in the scene before him, looking her up and down, and then he leans back over towards her and hikes her skirt up a bit, exposing her thighs and the lower part of her panties slightly. With a quick shrug and another thought, he hikes it up that much further, now totally exposing her underwear, and leaves her skirt there, satisfied with the look. He gives her a little kiss, more a peck than anything, and sits back in his seat once more, getting comfortable. He doesn't say anything at all, but this time he picks up his coffee and looks out the window, eyes back on the house, ignoring her for the moment.

Demi moans in frustration and wiggles around in her seat; not terribly hard though, as she knows she could realistically get out of her restraints, and that would wreck their fun. Instead she pulls against the soft ropes holding her captive, wiggling her body, and sliding her legs around on the seat seductively, turning herself on more and hopefully teasing him enough to make him give in and give her what she wants, what she knows they both want.

Adam watches the house for a few more minutes, sipping his coffee some more, now cold, before setting it back down in the cup holder and taking in the scene beside him once more; her tied up in the passenger seat, spread and horny for him. It had been hard to ignore her, even for a few minutes, trying not to look at her out of the corner of his eye. He leans down and kisses her again, opening her lips with his tongue and pushing his way inside her mouth, eager for her. He runs one hand through her hair, touching her lightly, while the other reaches down between her spread legs and cups her hot mound, wet even through her panties.

She moans loudly into his mouth, thrusting her hips up against the feel of his hand holding her firmly, aching for more. Surprisingly, he is happy to oblige, and she feels the tips of his fingers along the edges of her underwear, tugging at them and pulling them to the side. Suddenly she is exposed completely, her wet pussy lips on display for any passerby and for him to do as he pleases with. She thrusts her hips upwards again, desperate for more, loving feeling helpless to him.

He uses his first two fingers to spread her lips wide, letting the cool air caress her most intimate of places. Then ever so slowly, he rubs the tip of his middle finger over her clit, causing her to moan again, and her hips to lift. He pulls his face away, breaking their kiss, and watches both her face and the scene between her legs as he begins to touch her with his fingers.

He traces circles around her sensitive clit and the hood a few times, watching as her hips thrust up in rhythm with his touch, before slowly sliding his first two fingers back down along her very wet slit. They reach her aching hole and slide in with no resistance, as she is soaking wet from his teasing and she almost jumps off the seat with her hips to meet his touch.

Adam laughs at her eagerness, but he doesn't slow down; instead he slides his first and second finger in and out of her at a fast pace, making sure to curl them inside on occasion so he can hit her sweet spot, making her cry out. He does this for a few minutes, loving the feel of her slippery lips clinging to him, before slowly removing them and sliding back up to her clit, and rubbing circles around it again, this time harder.

Demi moans and thrashes around in her seat, tugging on the soft ropes, trying to move her body closer to him, wanting more. Adam watches her face closely now, listening to her breathing too, watching for signs that she's growing closer to orgasm. He slides his fingers back inside her again, hitting her g spot right off the hop, and she cries out once more and begins almost humping his hand with her hips, her legs squeezing his hand tightly.

He chooses that moment to pull his hand away, withdrawing completely and sitting back in his seat. Demi moans in frustration and tugs against her restraints a little harder this time, trying to pull her arms free. She's practically soaking, so close to cumming, and is desperate for him. "Please, babe," she begs him, thrusting her hips again, "please don't leave me like this."

Adam totally ignores this scene, even though it kills him more than it did last time, and he picks up his cold coffee instead and turns his attention back to the house they're watching. He's putting up a really good front; his cock is rock hard, and he is dying to make her cum all over his hand, but damned if he's going to let her know that. He's going to make her wait.

Her cries fall on deaf ears for a few more minutes, although he is sneakily watching her thrust and moan and beg out of the corner of his eye, before he finally sets his coffee down once more. He looks over at her, and she says to him, only half-jokingly, "You know, you're getting far too much enjoyment out of torturing me like this." "You have no idea what torturing really is," he replies with a wink, and licks his lips.

Demi feels her entire body shudder, and her pussy grows even more wet; it's now a constant throbbing between her legs. She forces herself to relax, and take a deep breath, even though she's aching for him, and she awaits patiently for what he wants to do with her. He leans down and kisses her once more, lightly this time, more passionately than before. He runs his fingers over her lower lips teasingly, gently, rubbing her everywhere. He finally parts her wet lower lips again and finds her hole and slides two fingers deep inside, wiggling them, causing her to moan all over again.

He finger fucks her hard this time, taking her, holding her tiny body tightly, feeling her shudder against him. He thinks about teasing her again; about bringing her to the brink of orgasm and then leaving her to suffer one more time, knowing that it won't take long to get her there. She's already dripping wet and close from her last delayed orgasm. But Demi seems to know this is coming, and she starts thrusting her hips upwards again and begging him to let her cum. Pleading with him. "Please, don't stop this time. I just want to cum, please make me cum." She begs desperately, her legs clinging to him tightly, trying to hold his hand there.

Adam doesn't stop this time; he does exactly what she asks of him. He pushes his fingers harder in and out of her, rubbing her g spot, feeling her juices leak all over his hand as she gets closer. He kisses her urgently, pushing his tongue deep inside of her mouth, trying to muffle her moans of enjoyment.

Demi feels herself growing closer and closer and prays he doesn't stop again. She's pulling against the ropes, feeling the soft material dig into her wrists, and all but flying off the seat at him with her hips, helping push his fingers as far inside of her as they can go. His tongue is all over hers, his lips hot against her own, and she moans into his mouth, crying out for him, wanting it all.

He picks up speed, breaking their kiss and pulling away from her just enough to watch her face as his fingers touch her in expert places and push her over the edge, forcing the orgasm she begged him for. Her eyes close and her body arches against the seat as her hips thrust up against him. He feels her pussy walls clench and squeeze his fingers tightly, milking him, as her legs clamp down around his wrists, pinning his hand into her as she cums all over him, her juices dripping down his hand and onto the seat below her.

Adam leaves Demi shaking and breathing heavily in the seat, still tied, eyes closed, while he pulls away from her. Just as she began to orgasm, there was movement from the house that had caught his attention, and it took all he had to bring her to that final orgasm while still trying to case the joint and figure out what was going on, which is what they were supposed to be here doing in the first place, and not fooling around like they always end up doing.

He watches what looks like the husband preparing to leave with suitcases, a day ahead of schedule, and in the middle of the night. Instant red flags go up for Adam. And as he looks through the binoculars to get a closer look, it doesn't appear that the wife is packing up or going with them. In fact, it looks like they may be having a fight right now. This is not good.

As he grows more and more distracted by the scene unfolding in front of them, and what he's supposed to do about it, or what this is going to mean for their heist, he forgets about Demi, who is struggling and pulling against her restraints in the passenger seat, still spread open and tied up, and long come down from her orgasm now.

"Adam, hey, earth to Adam" Demi says, calling out his name a few times and trying to get his attention, still pulling at the ropes holding her arms behind the seat, trying to free her wrists. "Are you going to untie me? Please? What's going on? Babe?"

He half ass laughs at her, but he never takes his eyes off the house, or sets the binoculars down; he never even looks at Demi. "You know, a few minutes ago you were all but begging to be where you are now sweetheart, you women can't make up your mind." he says with a smirk, and she feels her face flush as she realizes how exposed she is right now, still unable to get her hands free, panties pulled to the side and skirt hiked up high, everything on display.

She tries to pull her legs together and hide herself a little bit, squirming around in her seat, when suddenly Adam leans over her again, pushing her legs wide open once more by her thighs and this time leaning down and placing his face close to her pussy, his breath hot on her already wet and sensitive areas.

He leans down further still and spreads her lips with one hand and runs his tongue along the length of her, tasting her juices and her cum, listening to her moan and gasp for air. He can't see what's going on at the house from here though, bending down low with the dashboard in his way, so after a few gently sucks and licks around her hard nub he sits back up in his seat and resumes watching the house, but keeps his hand on her, and slowly begins to run his fingers up and down her wet folds. "Just be quiet and stay put, and enjoy yourself," he says to her with another sideways smirk, not taking his eyes off the windshield.

Demi can tell something is wrong; Adam's whole demeaner has changed and the atmosphere in the car is significantly different, his nerves are clearly shot, and something is bothering him, a lot. Even the tone of his voice is off. But he obviously doesn't want to talk about it, as he still has her tied up and his fingers are keeping themselves occupied with her, so she sighs and lays back in the seat, enjoying his touch. He always knows just how to touch her, what makes her feel good and what makes her toes curl, and that gives her a great distraction.

This time though, it's as if he is taking his aggressions, his worries, whatever is wrong right now, out on her. Two of his fingers slide down and push their way inside of her again, roughly, all the way inside and she gasps loudly at the way he takes her. He wiggles them deeply around inside of her, and then brings them back out before pushing them all the way back in, again and again. The quickness of his pace, and this new found demanding need of her body from him turns her on immensely, and Demi cries out loud as her hips rise up to meet him and she pushes herself back against the seat.

Adam brings her to another orgasm, urgently this time, totally out of control and out of character for him, but his mind is lost. He never takes his eyes off the house in front of him the entire time his hands have their way with her, and he doesn't see her body shake and shudder for him as she begins to cum. He is a million miles away.

Her moans and little mewing sounds she's making, and her legs clenched tightly around his wrists while her vaginal walls squeeze him tight, is just enough to break him out of his trance for a moment. He leans down and gives her a long, deep, slow kiss, pushing his tongue into her mouth, tasting her and leaving the hint of her own juices in her mouth. He pulls away and reaches around her and unties her wrists and drops the rope behind her seat without a word, and then sits back in his own seat and looks back at the house, not even acknowledging her, completely self-absorbed.

Feeling frustrated with the change in their situation, Demi sits up in a huff and starts to get herself settled in her seat while fixing her panties and skirt and adjusting her shirt. Once she's feeling back to normal, no longer exposed and on display, and she's put her seat back into the upright position, she takes a minute to look over the house their watching, and then over at Adam. He is stone faced and still staring at the house, not giving her the time of day. She clears her throat, but he doesn't even seem to notice her, so she turns her attention back to the house to try and figure out what's going on herself, and why he's got himself all worked up.

She can see a little bit of movement in the windows and a flickering of lights, and it seems like they are getting ready to go, as she can see someone going to and from the house to the car and into the garage a few times. It may be a day early, but they're still leaving, so she doesn't really understand what he's worried about. She can't help but wonder if it's her, if she's done something wrong to him, or around him, or even towards this heist and if that's why he's upset.

Demi takes a deep breath, holding it for a second before releasing it, and finds a little bit of courage inside of her, even though she's feeling nervous. She mentally scolds herself for feeling that way, knowing that it's just her being insecure, what else is new, and that she's probably just making a mountain out of a molehill, then she turns to him and asks him if everything is ok.

She could almost laugh; for all the worry she's putting herself through, he still doesn't even acknowledge her presence, he is so lost in his own head and his own thoughts that she may as well not even be here with him. She takes another breath and leans towards him a bit and shakes his knee slightly, getting his attention and snapping him out of his thoughts. "Hey, Adam, what's going on?" She says once she knows that he's actually listening to her.

Except she still doesn't get the answer, or the reaction from him, that she's hoping for. He just grunts at her and tells her that he doesn't think the wife is leaving with the husband, and then he turns his attention back to the house in front of them and shuts her back out again.

Demi instantly grows concerned. "What do you mean the wife isn't leaving? How do you know this?" When he doesn't answer her right away, she turns her own attention back to the house again and tries to see things the way he's seeing it, but all she sees is movement. She feels really lost.

"Adam? Seriously, how do you know this?" She asks once more, almost begging this time, trying to get some sort of response from him.

Suddenly Adam seems to grow extremely irritated, and agitated, and she doesn't know what's happening anymore, but it feels like it's directed at her. "I just know, ok? I know what I know. Stop it. No more questions." He starts the car in a huff, throws his seatbelt on and drives off, away from the subdivision and back towards the hotel, without waiting for her to respond, or for her to even put her own belt on.

She throws it on as they drive, clipping it in while her thoughts race just as fast as Adam is driving through the city. What is going on? How does he know the wife isn't leaving? What does that mean? For them, and for the heist? She can't help but feel like there is more to this than she realizes, more to this than he's telling her, and she's terrified that she's done something somehow to set him off, to cause all of this.

Adam cranks the radio as he drives, not just to drown out anything that Demi may have to say next, but also to try to drown out the thoughts that are flying around in his head, that are freaking him out and making him question the whole heist. Everything just changed so fast, and he can't seem to process it all at once. One minute he was enjoying the feel of her soft silky body under his fingertips, and the next his mind was a mess as he tried to figure out what was going on in the house in front of him, and what he was supposed to do now.

What were they going to do if the wife didn't leave? How were they going to pull off this heist? Have they done all of this for nothing?

Chapter Eleven

Adam still hasn't spoken a single word to her by the time they drive closer to the hotel, and now his entire posture has changed as well, into one of tense thoughts and anger about to boil over; his hands grip the wheel tightly, and he's sitting straight up in his seat, never taking his eyes off the road, his knuckles white from the pressure.

Demi has grown more and more concerned and more and more nervous and insecure the closer they've got to the hotel. Her mind is a complete mess with one thousand thoughts flying around in there, and it isn't helping that Adam is refusing to speak to her or answer any of her questions. The longer he stays quiet, the more drawn into her head she becomes, until she's a total mess inside by the time they reach the hotel and Adam parks the car.

She watches silently from the passenger seat as he gets out of the car and shuts the door. He doesn't even look back at her as he walks towards the stairs to their room, he doesn't even wait for her. With a heavy sigh, she unclips her seat belt and hurries to follow, feeling cold in the dark, late-night air and anxious to get inside and get into the shower, and put a little distance between them for a while, wanting to clear her head.

Adam unlocks the door to their room, and Demi all but pushes past him, grabbing a towel and heading directly for the bathroom, locking the door behind her, needing to be alone. Adam barely registers her movements, he is still so caught up in his own thoughts about the heist, and the change in plans, he probably wouldn't have even noticed if she didn't make it back into the hotel room with him. He does wonder briefly why she's in such a hurry, but then the thought is gone. Then he grabs himself a beer from the mini fridge, cracks it, and heads out to the balcony to give his friend a call so that they can touch base and maybe make a new plan, so that Adam can settle his head a bit. He also needs some fresh air, and to get out of that cramped car and hotel room with everything about the heist right there in front of his face. He needs a bit of a break himself.

From inside the bathroom, Demi hears the door to the balcony open and shut as Adam makes his way outside. She is feeling so overwhelmed and uncertain, and the sound of the door cracks something inside of her. It sounds like him leaving and shutting her out. The flood gates open and the tears begin to fall, hot and fast, and she stifles sobs as she slumps against the bathroom door and lets herself feel what she's feeling.

She knows that she's most likely just being emotional. She has a habit of over thinking everything, and relationships are so new to her. She is constantly wondering if she's done something wrong, or if there was something else that she should have done instead, or that she's making a great big mess of things. And in most of those cases, she ends up being wrong, and she's done everything perfectly, and when she does confide in him about how she's feeling, he just laughs and kisses her and tells her not to worry so much. Most of the time.

Demi takes a couple of slow, deep breaths, willing herself to calm down a little bit and for her mind to stop racing. Sitting on the floor crying, getting herself all worked up over total speculation in her head is not going to help anything, and she knows it. It's never helped her before. Slowly, she picks herself up off the bathroom tiles and stands and stretches, taking a few more deep breaths to steady herself further. Then she leans over the shower controls and turns the water on very hot before stripping out of her clothes and jumping in, hoping to wash all her cares and stress away.

She's in the shower for so long that the water starts to lose some of its heat, and by then she's come down from her emotional outburst. Now she just feels foolish, exhausted and drained from the day in entirety. She turns off the water and steps out of the shower, wrapping herself in a towel and slowly drying off her hair. All she wants now is to curl up into bed beside him and pretend none of this happened and go to sleep.

Demi comes back into the hotel room from the bathroom to see Adam sitting on the bed, fidgeting with a beer in one hand and his ghost phone in the other. Her breath catches on a lump in her throat at the sight of him sitting there, and when he looks up at her, her knees go weak. He is so handsome, she thinks to herself, and she's crazy about him. She had been feeling so calm and sure of herself when she had walked out of the bathroom, but now, standing here in front of him in only a towel, drained from her emotional outburst, everything inside of her begins to fall apart and she has no idea what she's supposed to say to him now. Finding a balance here, finding her place in this relationship, trying to figure out everything that's going on, whether she's just being emotional or not; it's all overwhelming her.

She doesn't need to know what to say though, because Adam starts speaking almost immediately once she's out of the bathroom and standing there in front of him. He is still so self-absorbed in what's going on, so focused on the heist, that he hasn't even noticed her off mood, or that it looks like she spent the better part of her time in the shower crying and sad. He hardly even notices that she's only clad in a towel.

"I've been doing some back-ground checking on a few things, and making some phone calls," he starts off, "and I confirmed what I had already suspected while we were back at the house. His wife isn't leaving with him on this trip. Her flight was cancelled last night, and he's already gone and booked himself into a hotel room early before he leaves. Something is going on with them, and I don't like it."

Demi can't help herself, she moans in almost embarrassment at what he's saying to her, and damn near drops the towel she's still holding around her naked body. The sound she makes causes Adam to really look up at her, and the expression on her face confuses him. "What's wrong?" He asks her, growing concerned, tossing his phone over on the bed and patting the space beside him, indicating for her to sit with him.

She laughs, her nervous, embarrassed laughter, and takes a seat on the bed next to him, really feeling ridiculous now. She knew she had been right from the start, but she also knows that she's terrible with this relationship business, and she let herself get stuck in her head. She tries to cut herself a little bit of slack. "I'm sorry, I feel really dumb," she starts off, playing with a strand of her hair. "I was feeling really insecure back there in the car, I thought I had done something wrong or something to upset you. Or that maybe I did something to affect the heist. And you wouldn't even talk to me, or even really look at me, so that didn't help. I got so caught up inside my head, I made a huge deal out of something that wasn't even an issue at all. What else is new."

Adam can't help but let out a laugh himself, realizing her feelings have nothing to do with the heist whatsoever, and that this is not the first time that's happened. And he feels awful, because he knows he didn't help the situation with his one-track mind; hell, he hadn't even noticed anything was wrong with Demi, or really noticed that she was sitting here beside him, wet in a towel. He needs to get out of his head a little bit more.

"I'm so sorry babe, I never meant to make you feel that way at all. Some of this is definitely my fault too, even if you think you overreacted about nothing." He replies to her, and wraps an arm around her toweled body, pulling her closer to him and kissing her on the forehead. "I'm glad you talked to me about it though, instead of keeping it to yourself." he says into the top of her head, smelling her freshly washed hair, loving the scent of her and the warm feeling of her so close to him. "I'm really lucky to have found you, you know." "I know," she replies jokingly with a wink, and nudges him lightly.

"Why don't you get some comfortable pjs on, and I will run to the vending machine for some late-night munchies and drinks," he says to her, "and then we can snuggle up in bed and talk about what we're going to do next, maybe watch some TV and then call it a night? What do you say?"

"I say that's a fantastic idea," she says to him, leaning forward and kissing him lightly on the lips, feeling happy, relieved and very content with the moment.

Chapter Twelve

Bright and early the next morning, and far too early for Demi's liking, the pair are sitting in the far back booth of a quiet mom and pop breakfast shop, out of earshot of anyone else, talking quietly about their plans. Adam had insisted they get up early even though they'd had such a late night the night before, because they have a lot of thinking and talking and prepping to do, after they figure out all the changes that need to be made. He had sweetened the deal by telling her they could nap in the afternoon, and so she's agreed to the early start, while grudgingly.

Demi chews on a piece of bacon slowly while she watches steam rise from her mug of coffee, listening to Adam talk. He's been going over and over the same changes of plans and the same routine again and again, going around in circles, and with how little sleep she's running on, it's enough to grate on her nerves. She keeps hoping that her coffee is going to kick in soon and wake her up enough that she stops feeling so crabby and irritated, and ready to yell at him, "Let's just call it off already!!"

The fact of the matter is, they have had this conversation already, and will very likely be having it again, and soon, and probably again after that, but it didn't end well last night, and probably won't this time, or the time after that either. Demi sees no real reason why they need to even preform the heist anymore, if there are going to be complications like this. She has no attachments to the plan, and money has never been an issue for her anyway. Her only concern is the thrill; and that she can get from any other robbery or gas and go they want to pull off, and she just doesn't understand why Adam can't let this whole thing go.

However, Adam is invested in this, and he isn't willing to go down without a fight. They have traveled all the way here, they have done all this planning and preparation, he's involved his friend, and taken a lot of risks to pull this off. This is a huge thrill, but he also knows this is a huge payoff as well, and it's just too easy to let this chance pass them by if he can help it, if he can still find a way to make it work. Even if that entails arguing a bit with Demi to get her to see his side.

Adam takes a long sip of his coffee, letting it warm him and calm his nerves slightly, and then he keeps talking. "We've still got to take a chance and see, it's simply too good of an opportunity, it's calling out to me. Something will work out in our favor, I can feel it, I don't even care if that's crazy. I know there is nothing listed on any of the logs or social media sites that I can find, but I bet she has something planned anyway and she's going to leave the house or leave town entirely herself. This is going to work out for us. We just have to have some faith."

Demi can't help herself, her moodiness has overcome her, and she snaps back a response, eager to play devil's advocate, and pop a hole in his plans. "And what if she doesn't, hey? What if her plan while her husband is away is to sit around eating snacks and watching movies in her pajamas, and not moving from the couch all weekend? Or, better yet, what if her plan is to have a bunch of girlfriend's over for a wine and spa weekend, and the house is full of women, eyes all over the place, no way for us to even get on the property, let alone inside to perform the heist?"

Adam is a little put off by her tone and the attitude she's throwing at him, it being so unlike her, and the two of them begin to get into a bit of an argument in the corner booth, in hushed whispered voices. Adam keeps insisting that the wife will leave, or something will work out in their favor, and Demi keeps shutting all his ideas down and poking holes in everything he says, eager to make him see that this isn't going to work.

"I'm starting to think you don't even want to do this anymore," Adam says to her with a huffed sigh, and Demi lets out a small laugh and rolls her eyes at him. "Well, no shit Sherlock, if it's not going to work out, then it's not going to work out. It's time for us, well, you, to accept that and move on to something else."

The waitress comes by and takes their plates, still mostly filled with food, and very empty coffee mugs, and leaves the cheque for them on the table and walks away. Even she can feel the tension in the air between the two lovers and isn't eager to stick around any longer than she needs to.

"It *is* going to work out," he replies angerly, tossing some bills down on the table to pay for their breakfast, and stuffing his wallet back into his jeans as he stands up. "But we aren't going to know that for sure until we give it a shot and try it. And we aren't going to know how to adjust our plans until we know for sure what's going on, so we may as well just go and wing it and hope for the best. It's going to work out." He says that last bit with authority, not expecting anymore argument from her.

"I think that's a stupid idea," Demi mutters under her breath, standing up and throwing her coat on, slowly getting ready to leave. "Oh, and do you have a better idea, besides throwing in the towel and calling it quits?" He retorts back, putting his own coat on.

Demi doesn't have any other ideas, and she is tired, and tired of arguing with him. She just wants to go back to the hotel, take a nap, and just like he says, see where this thing takes them. She doesn't feel like she has any other choice at this point. She tells him no, she doesn't, and they walk back to the hotel in silence, both of their thoughts on the night of preparation ahead, and what may lie in wait for them.

Chapter Thirteen

Even after they've arrived back at the hotel, Demi is still feeling off and moody about the entire ordeal. She truly doesn't think things are going to work out for them if they just wing it, and she cannot shake the feeling that something is going to go wrong for them, nor can they continue to argue about this any longer, she is completely exhausted from it.

They pack and prepare a few things that they think they may need for their first trial run tonight with little talking happening between them, and the atmosphere in the hotel room is slightly tense. They are both feeling tired still as well, so after things are as ready as they can be, with a few bags prepped and ready over by the door, Adam suggests that the two of them take a nap and catch up on some rest.

Walking down the hall to the vending machine, they grab a few snacks and drinks and then head back to their hotel room. Snuggling up in the bed together, still not talking much but feeling less anxiety between them, the pair snack on some munchies and then doze off while watching a nature documentary on the hotel tv.

Demi awakes a few hours later to movement between her thighs, forcing her legs apart, and she feels Adam crawl between them. At some point while she's been sleeping her pants have been removed, and so have her panties, and the bedsheets caress her bare-naked skin as he moves beneath them. Then she feels Adam's hands on her, his fingers slowly spreading her pussy lips apart as his tongue pushes its way into her hot, wet slit, tasting her, waking her up fully.

She throws her head back against the pillow and moans out loud, laying back and relaxing her body, letting him have his way with her, letting him make her feel good. After all the tension and anxiety that's been growing between them the last little while, a few orgasms are exactly what she needs, are what they both need.

Adam's tongue pushes its way in and out of her tight little hole, tasting all her juices, making her squirm and whither around on the bed under his touch, wanting more. Two of his fingers slide in under his tongue and he slowly starts to finger fuck her softly, teasing her, moving his mouth upwards to her hard nub. He lightly licks her clit a few times, making her jump and cry out, before taking it between his lips and gently sucking and pulling on it, while still wiggling and thrusting his fingers deeper and deeper inside of her, touching all the spots she loves.

It isn't going to take her long to orgasm this way, and she doesn't hesitate to tell him so between her moans and soft little cries of ecstasy. That only turns Adam on even more, and he picks up speed, sucking on her clit harder and sliding his fingers faster in and out of her, eager to make her cum all over his hand and mouth, dying to taste her.

Demi reaches up behind her and grabs the pillow and pulls it around her, gripping it tightly, as her body squirms underneath him, hips thrusting upwards, desperate for more. She feels herself gasping, and her heart begin to race, as the feelings get more and more intense and Adam brings her closer and closer to orgasm. His fingers are in her, and then out of her, and in again, spreading her open, pushing against her g spot, slipping in her juices, as he continues his oral assault on her clit, and then everything overwhelms her, and she cries out, yelling his name, her legs pinning him and holding him close as she begins to orgasm.

She is still cumming, her body shaking and her tight pussy still pulsing, when suddenly Adam is on her, his body over top of hers, and his hard cock is thrusting its way deep inside her, parting her silky walls and pushing deep into her. Demi cries out again, loving the feeling of being filled by him, and reaches up and wraps her arms around him and pulls him down closer to her.

"Seemed like we could both use this," he says softly in her ear, leaning down even closer and pressing his chest against hers, his lips light against her neck. Demi doesn't say anything, she just moans and pulls him close, turning his face to hers and kissing him urgently. She slides her tongue against his lips, and he parts them for her, kissing her back just as eagerly and passionately, needing her, needing things to feel ok for a little while.

Their hands are all over each other's bodies, grabbing and holding and touching everywhere they can grab, not able to get enough of one another. Adam's hips press up against hers, over and over, sliding his cock in and out of her sweet tight opening, while she clings to him and pushes back hard against him, taking it all.

It doesn't take either of them long to cum this way; Demi having already came once and being so turned on and close to orgasm as it is, and Adam having woken up with a raging hard on and then gotten even more worked up from eating her out before they started having sex, which has turned more into them making love to one another. Demi feels herself getting closer and moans in his ear that she's going to cum again, while pressing herself against him and digging her nails lightly into his back, pulling him back into her, needing all of him.

Adam picks up speed, grabbing Demi by the waist with one hand and really giving it to her, harder, pushing her down into the bed beneath him as he kisses her deeply again, muffling the sound of her moans with his tongue and his lips. He feels her pussy contract around his rock-hard cock, milking him as she starts to cum, and that sets him over the edge. He feels himself release deep inside her, engulfed by her, as her body shudders under him, in his arms.

He kisses her gently a few more times, pulling away from her slowly, letting them both breathe and come back down from their sexual high. The tension between them is gone now, at least for the moment, and they snuggle up naked together, feeling normalcy seep between them once again. Demi loves being wrapped up in his arms, feeling safe and secure, and loved, and it doesn't take long for both of them to fall back asleep again, tired out from their sudden emotional and sexual release.

They wake up once more a few hours later, close to supper time, and they are absolutely starving. Adam makes plans for them to go grab dinner, and then stop for snacks, pop, coffee and food, as he watches Demi gets dressed. He's decided they're still going to case the place out tonight as planned, it's been settled, and now he just hopes that some sort of opportunity presents itself to them while they are there.

Chapter Fourteen

Later that evening finds the pair sitting in the car quietly, making small talk and munching on snacks, waiting for 11pm, which seems to be taking forever to roll around to on the clock. They plan to do their first walk around the area then, and then do another trip around the block and the property later, around 2am, and one final one before the sun comes up, pretending they're on an early morning stroll. They've made sure to come equipped with everything they need to tie themselves over for the night, while they stake and canvass the place out, and try to come up with a new plan of action.

Adam still has no ideas in mind, and Demi is trying very hard not to let that get to her again, now that they are really here, and still going through with this. Sitting around all night watching the place through binoculars, walking around the block a few times in the dark, and actually sneaking onto the property on foot, hoping for an idea to strike them, or for something to happen in their favor, just doesn't seem likely to her. As if the wife is just going to pack her bags and up and go away on her own vacation, leaving the place empty for them to do as they please. But, since there is finally peace between them again, and since they are cooped up in this car together for hours, she keeps her mouth shut, in no mood to start another fight.

The most eventful thing that happens all evening up until their first stroll is that the wife leaves the gate to the house open, although neither of them know if she does this by accident or if she's expecting company. There are security cameras around the gated entranceway anyway, but that doesn't matter to them at all. They don't plan to pass by that side of the street, and if all the information Adam's friend has given them holds up, (and so far, so good), they will be sneaking onto the property from the back of the lot, hidden from view of almost everything, in a more deserted area of the subdivision, where they hopefully won't be seen.

Eventually it reaches 11pm, and by then they're both itching to get out of the car and go for a walk to stretch their legs and enjoy some fresh air. Between all the driving, and all the stake outs and hotel stays they have done lately, Demi has learned to appreciate her time walking around out in the open, feeling free, at least for the time being.

It is a calm and quiet night, with very little wind, and no movement from the surrounding trees. They're also in a quiet, richer area of town, the sound of traffic here is almost null, and the few houses here are dim and silent. They walk slowly, holding hands and taking in all the sights around them, not in any particular hurry or going in any specific way, simply looking around at everything. They do make sure they walk along the end of the property where they will enter later, but otherwise they walk mindlessly, just watching, and thinking.

The smell of flowers lingers in the night air. "It's really beautiful here," Demi comments softly, as they walk along a dimly lit stone front garden along the wall of someone's gated yard. "It sure is," Adam agrees, squeezing her hand a little and pulling her closer into him as they walk. "I wonder what it would be like to live in one of these houses and live a life like these people do." He says.

Demi suddenly finds herself laughing quietly, not being able to stop it, catching herself by surprise. Adam stops their walk for a moment, tugging on her hand. "What's so funny?" He asks. "It's just, I, just," she starts, stuttering, not able to get her thoughts together right away. "It's almost like I've forgotten that I lived in a beautiful house once, that this was my life. We've just been traveling and on the road for so long that I almost forget what it's like to have my own place again, what it's like to be settled, and have a place to call home."

What she says strikes a cord inside of him, and echoes thoughts that he himself has had while they've been on the road this past month or so, but he hasn't voiced to her. This seems like a good a time as any though, so he takes her hand and continues walking while he talks, not really knowing what he plans to say, but wanting to try to explain how he's feeling to her all the same.

"You know, I've had some very similar thoughts lately while we've been driving around seeing the sights and passing the time, although not quite about the living in a fancy house part, I've never lived in one of those, so you've got me beat there." They both share a laugh at his poor attempt at a joke, and he continues. "But what I've also been thinking is that we haven't really had a normal "relationship" per say, like we would have otherwise, in a sense that we didn't have our own places and were living our own lives, and then dated, and slowly began to live together, your tooth brush at my place, my work shirts at yours. Not that we haven't had a great time doing what we're doing, and made some awesome memories along the way, but I have certainly thought about what it would have been like to live with you that way in the beginning, and had a "normal" relationship, and not just packed everything we owned that was important to us into suitcases and hit the road for weeks on end, with no actual end destination in mind of what we are doing as our relationship grows."

Adam hadn't actually meant to ramble on like that, and he wasn't sure where that last part had come from either, about not knowing what their end game was as things progressed between them. To be honest, that was something he's thought about once or twice, or maybe more times than that, but that isn't something he had planned to talk about yet, at all. It had just slipped out.

"Well, it's not exactly like our relationship started off normally either, remember that, kidnapper," Demi says with a laugh, and then the conversation sort of ends there, both left with some things to think about.

They grow quiet as their walk winds up, each lost in their own thoughts now. Thoughts about their relationship, thoughts about what had already transpired between them, and what may happen in the future, their thoughts keeping them busy amongst themselves. It isn't awkward, or tense, it's just quiet as they are both thinking, but neither willing to share those thoughts yet with one another.

Just before they get back to the car, they both take turns popping into the bushes along the side of the road to relieve themselves before ducking back into the dark car again. There are no 24-hour stores or restaurants around here, and that's fine because Adam wouldn't have let them use one anyway, not wanting to draw any more attention to themselves than necessary. It is dark and forested and secluded down this end of the street where Adam has parked, and he feels fine about that decision, knowing that it's very likely no one will ever notice them or remember them.

They get cozy in the car this time, not quite sitting in their own seats, Demi stretched out with her legs draped across his lap, and his arms wrapped around her. They make small talk for a while, although it's just light chatter this time, nothing about relationships or what they had spoken about prior, neither of them wanting to get into any kind of heavy conversation while they're stuck in the car. They sip soft drinks and munch out on snacks for a while, watching the house through binoculars. When Demi checks the time to see about their next walk around, she is genuinely surprised to find that it's 2:10am, ten minutes past when they had planned to leave.

Time can pass by extremely fast when they are together, when things are happy and comfortable between them. They are both so happy in each other's company and seem to be able to talk for hours about everything and anything, without it ever feeling forced or awkward. Sometimes that isn't always a good thing though, like when they are on a time crunch, or have somewhere to be at a specific time, like now, and find they're behind schedule because of it.

Just as she's thinking it, Adam makes a remark himself about the time and how they need to get a move on as they're late, and she snaps out of her thoughts and they get to work. At Adam's insistence earlier, they had dressed in all black, but had worn colorful / normal light jackets and sweaters over top, and hats, so they didn't look *too* conspicuous while they walked around the neighborhood on their walk about before midnight. Now however, they ditched the outer layers and put on black jackets and sweaters and hats, hoping to blend into the darkness and not be noticed.

This time when they head out for a walk, they don't canvass the entire area for an hour like they did the last time. Instead, they take a quick look around for a moment to make sure no one seems to be out and about, who might be watching them, and then they head directly to the back of the property where they plan to make their way in.

Adam's friend had used to do property maintenance for the couple, and had let them know about a patched, re-patched and now in great need of repair part of the back-yard stone wall that was falling apart underneath an old oak tree. It would make the perfect ladder. They had seen the area earlier, and it looked like a simple entrance and exactly as he had described. So far tonight, their luck was holding out for them.

They reached the hole in the wall and took a moment to have one more look around to make sure they weren't being seen by anyone they could obviously see, maybe someone taking their dog for a late-night pee, or someone out for a god awful early morning jog. It was very late, or very early, depending on how you looked at the clock, and the few houses within sight were dark. For the most part, this area of the subdivision was quiet, dark empty backyards and no one around to be seen.

Demi approaches the wall first and places her hands up on the ledge for grip. Adam gives her a boost up, and she sits there for a moment, staying still and taking in the yard and having a much better look around now that she's been given a bird's eye view of the property. Between the light of the moon and the glow of the few house lights, the yard is lit in a pale white light, but there really isn't much to see. Some lawn decorations, a fountain, a few gorgeous gardens and bushes. The yard is as quiet and deserted as the rest of the yards on the street.

Demi climbs down the tree and begins to scale into the yard, landing on her feet softly as Adam now pulls himself up on the ledge and then drops down beside her, making it look much easier than she had. Luck is on their side on this side of the wall as well; the ground is sloped downwards in here, and the walls tower just high enough above their heads to offer protection from the street, so they can't be seen sneaking around by any passerby's.

Without a word, the pair begin to step lightly and slowly make their way towards the house, which is almost entirely dark except for the soft glow from a few windows close together, from what looks to be a dim night light and possibly the flickering of a TV from a bedroom. The rest of the house appears pitch black and shut up for the night.

The windows that are lit up are on the ground floor and easily accessible from the outside, with the shades open, which is perfect for them, and they creep up to one of the windows slowly, feeling like a pair of peeping toms. Adam runs the risk of looking first. He takes a deep breath, feeling his heart racing a mile a minute in his chest, hammering away, nervous and filled with anxiety about what he may find. He stands up tall and glances around the window frame and into the bedroom, prepared for whatever.

Adam lets out the breath he hasn't even realized he's been holding since he sucked it in. He also doesn't know what he's having anxiety over; he guesses he just imagined something other than this. He sees the wife tucked into bed, the TV on, a phone laid on the bed beside her and a book in her hand. There is a glass of wine sitting on the nightstand beside the bed. It's pretty much exactly what he would expect Demi to be doing if they lived together and he had to go out of town for the weekend. He feels a stitch of panic begin to tighten in his chest. He doesn't think she's going anywhere, and he isn't coming up with any real ideas about how they'll pull this heist off if she is in the house. He is lost as to what to do next.

He steps back and lets Demi have a look for herself, for all the good that is going to do them. He can feel his mood starting to switch, turning miserable and he hates it, but he still can't stop himself from saying in a hoarse whisper, "It certainly doesn't look like the wife is going anywhere anytime soon." Demi doesn't say anything to him in reply, she just steps back from the window once she's had a look, keeping her opinions of what she saw to herself, and stands there waiting for the next part of their plan. She doesn't want to push him.

With a nod of his head towards the back of the house, the pair make their way silently along the property, towards the garage, and then around it. Along the way, they pass the side entrance to the garage, with the keypad tucked off to the left on the wall. That's the way they have planned to enter the house, with the code Adam's friend provided, but that doesn't seem like a likely option if the wife is still in the house, sitting up late watching TV and reading books with a glass of wine, just waiting to bust them at any moment.

They make their way back towards the glowing lights of the windows to the wife's room, this time from the other side of the house, taking in all the details of the house and the property that they can in the pale moon light. Full circle leads them right back to the window, and they take turns having another peek, seeing that nothing has changed in the time it's taken them to go around the place.

Adam feels awful; a tight, sick feeling has formed at the pit of his stomach. His thoughts are starting to snowball, and he can't stop the anxiety and stress that's creeping in fast. The likelihood is that all of this has been for nothing, and they won't be able to go through with it. Or, everything will go wrong when they do, and they could end up with a lot more on their plates than just the excitement of a jewelry heist to add to their list of naughty things they've done. He hates to admit that Demi may have been right all along; they didn't need to do this, and they should just pack up and call it quits while they still can.

However, when he glances over at Demi, he sees a look on her face that he just can't quite read. It looks like Demi is stumped, or confused about something, or trying to make sense of something she's thinking about. There are definitely some wheels turning in there anyway. He reaches out and caresses her arm, and it almost takes her a moment to focus back in and turn to look at him. She certainly was deep in thought about something. He gestures towards the car, indicating that they walk back, but she shakes her head and holds up her finger to him; she wants one more minute.

Demi takes another look into the bedroom window, and gazes at the wife one last time, not feeling that peeping tom feeling that Adam gets, but rather feeling a whole mixture of emotions, and one wild, crazy idea. Now is not the time for discussing that though, she needs more time to think about it, and then a much better place to talk it over. She turns away from the window, and nods to Adam, and the two of them make their way back across the dimly lit backyard, towards the stone wall and the tree, and their way out.

Adam climbs up first, and after making sure the coast is still clear, he helps Demi up and over, and the two of them climb back down. They make their way back to the car in total silence, not even holding hands or walking that close together, each alone in their heads with their own thoughts. Adam can't help but feel this overwhelming sense of defeat, and what almost feels like depression, and he walks with a slump, brooding walk.

Adam unlocks the car and they get inside, not saying a word. The car is cold from their absence, and they bundle up in their outer clothes, not wanting to turn it on and have the rumble of the engine or the lights raise any attention to them. They go back to watching the house, not talking to each other still, a tension growing in the car. Adam doesn't want to talk. He doesn't want to admit they can't do this, and he doesn't want to admit that she's right. He's feeling stubborn, and the longer he stews on his thoughts, the worse it seems to get.

Except that every time he glances over at Demi, she seems lost in thought, and it almost looks like she's scheming, or planning. She's up to something, he knows it. *She* definitely doesn't seem upset, or defeated, or like she has to admit *she* is wrong and has to give up, he thinks bitterly to himself.

The silence, the darkness, and his thoughts spiraling out of control start to get the best of Adam, and he snaps out of nowhere around 4am and says that they're going to call it a night, almost an hour earlier than they had planned originally, and without doing their final walk around. But there is absolutely nothing happening here; the lights went out a while ago, and the wife went to bed, and now he and Demi are just sitting in this dark, cold car, lost in their own thoughts, driving themselves crazy. Or, at least, he is, and it gets worse the longer they sit here.

The drive back to the hotel is also silent, but at least driving gives Adam something to concentrate on other than his thoughts, and Demi. Demi is starting to rub on his nerves, and he doesn't even know why. If she isn't upset, and isn't looking defeated, maybe she has a plan, and that should make him happy. But right now, Adam can't seem to get over this feeling of failure, and he is ready to call it a night, not wanting to hash anything out with her, wanting to hide from it all.

Chapter Fifteen

The pair wake up around lunch time the next day, snuggled up in their hotel bed, feeling groggy and a bit rough from their very late night, and all the emotional turmoil going on inside their heads. They cuddle for a few minutes before they get out of bed, but neither are in the mood for sex, or even for talking to each other much yet; their thoughts are elsewhere, preoccupied with the robbery that is supposed to happen tonight, and if it's even going to happen tonight, and what they're going to do next, one way or another.

They take turns showering and getting dressed slowly and make themselves feel a little more human as they wake up. Then they set out for a walk down to the corner coffee shop for coffee and some take out breakfast, muffins and egg sandwiches, and then they just keep walking. They walk a little way until they reach the river and find a secluded spot in the morning sun to sit and have their breakfast and take a little time for themselves.

Adam is still feeling very grumpy and moody about the whole thing, unable to shake his feelings from the night before. His heart feels heavy, and he's about ready to tuck his tail between his legs and admit defeat. After they had been there up close and on foot, and saw what they'd saw, he's got a pretty good idea that tonight will be more of the same, and that won't work for them at all. They aren't going to be able to break into her house with her sitting right there, drinking wine and watching TV. He hates that he's about to admit that they don't need to do this, and it's time to move on, but he's ready to let it go, as angry and miserable as it makes him.

Demi is feeling conflicted too, but for very different reasons. Unbeknownst to Adam, she has been coming up with a plan of her own, thinking it over and over all night and morning, but she doesn't know if he will like it, or go for it, or if he'll judge her over it. She doesn't know what it will do to their relationship. It's wild and crazy and not like her at all, but it came to her out of nowhere while they stood at the wife's window last night, and now she can't shake the thought. She feels that it's at least worth talking over, because she thinks it's crazy enough to work.

Sitting there sipping their morning coffee, taking in the sunshine, they can each tell that the other is distracted, and heavy hearted, not there in the moment, but neither of them know how, or where to begin to talk to the other, so time drags on for a little while longer as they sit in silence and watch the water pass by.

The longer they sit there in silence though, and the longer this drags on, the more Demi begins to freak out inside her head, her plan and all her what ifs spinning around in circles, driving her nuts. She's so nervous, and her anxiety is through the roof, she can barely sit still beside him. She doesn't know where to start talking, with all her thoughts jumbled around causing her to feel so torn and confused, and so in the end, it's Adam who ends up speaking first.

"I don't think we should go forward with the heist anymore," he blurts out in a huge rush, and then lets out a giant sigh of relief, having been holding in a breath he didn't realize he'd been holding, so scared to actually speak those words out loud. "I really don't know what we're going to do about the wife. It doesn't seem like she's going to go away anywhere, nor does she seem to be much of a social person, and she's a night owl. I just can't see any way that we would be able to pull this off, she is a giant road block in our plans, and one we can't get rid of."

What he says is the total opposite of what she has in mind, it catches her off guard. Demi doesn't say anything in response to this right away. In fact, she doesn't say anything for so long that Adam starts to wonder if she even heard him, or if she's lost in her own thoughts somewhere, but then she clears her throat, and looks at him hesitantly, and then out at the river. "Maybe I have an idea," she says in a small voice.

Something about the way she says that, while not looking at him, instead staring out into the water and fidgeting with her coffee cup and picking at the lid, has peeked Adam's interest more than whatever her actual idea is. He knew she was up to something, but her reaction right now has him extremely curious. He waits for her to talk, not wanting to push her, but dying to know what she's been thinking about, what she's got hidden up her sleeve.

After a few more agonizing minutes of watching her silently, his thoughts racing and his curiosity on over drive, she finally speaks. "Maybe I could seduce her, and keep her busy," she almost whispers under her breath, so low he barely hears her, and then she waits nervously for his reaction.

Adam is so startled by what she's just said that he does this laughing cough thing that almost ends in him choking on a sip of coffee. What she's said is the last thing he'd ever thought about, he just wasn't expecting it, and the thought gets him laughing all over again, once he's caught his breath. It was the furthest thing from how he ever thought this heist would work itself out. "What, uh, come again?" He says, making sure he's heard her right.

Now it's Demi's turn to let out a big sigh of a breath that she didn't know she'd been holding, so worried about telling him what she'd been thinking, worried about him judging her or thinking she was crazy. But now that she can see that he isn't mad or jealous right off the hop, and he's at least half interested, she decides to feel him out with her idea. She takes a deep breath and starts talking about all the things she's been thinking about, and the plan she's half ass been forming in her head.

"I know that sounds, a little wild and crazy, but maybe I could seduce her, distract her and keep her occupied while you go in without me and still pull off the heist. Just, hear me out. From what I saw last night, when we were looking into the window, that wasn't their master bedroom, that was the guest room. And she looked lonely, and sad, and like she hasn't had any fun in a long time. And you said it looked like they'd had a fight. I bet money on the fact that they are having problems with their marriage, and things haven't been good in a while. That's why she's not staying in their bedroom while he's gone. That's why she's sleeping in the guest bedroom and looks like she's at home in a funk.

I was thinking, if I showed up at the house for some reason, which we would have to figure out before hand and perfect that part of the plan, and then convince her to let me in and have a glass or two of wine with me, I think the rest would happen fairly easily. A friendly chat, a little alcohol to loosen the mood, we start having fun, and you take advantage of the fact that I'm taking advantage of her, and you rob the place. We meet back at the car, once you're long gone and her and I are done our fun, and we ride off clean into the sunset together, still rich with jewelry and money, and high on the excitement of actually pulling this heist off."

She ends this long babble with an awkward little laugh, having been unsure how that was really supposed to end, just opening up to him and spewing out all her thoughts. And she's so unsure what he's really going to think of her plan, and of her, for thinking it up in the first place, or how he'd even feel about her being with a woman. She takes a sip of her coffee and anxiously waits for him to say something, anything, in response, time feeling like it's stopped while she waits.

Adam's not even sure he heard that right, and it takes him a moment, sitting there watching the water pass in silence, to absorb everything that she's said. It sounds like something right out of a porno movie, and with a laugh, he can't help but tell her as much. That seems to break the tension between them, and she laughs too, and leans in next to him, cuddling up, feeling slightly more relaxed now that she's gotten that off her chest.

Demi takes a few more sips of her coffee, and since he hasn't said anything past the porn comment, she continues. "For real though, this is something that I have been giving a lot of thought to since we were there last night. It kept me up tossing and turning all night and was the first thing I thought of again when I woke this morning. I can't get the idea out of my head. And I think, as nutty as it sounds, that it just might work. You let me be with a woman for one night, while you go ahead and preform the heist we had planned, and at the end of it all, we end up with a massive score. I say everyone wins in this scenario, well, maybe except the husband."

They both laugh at this joke, but Adam's head is a spinning mess, with everything she's told him going around and around in circles. Demi sounds like she has put a lot of thought into this, and she's very serious, but, *is* she serious? And could something as crazy as this, something that really does sound like it's straight out of an adult film, really work? It's not like they have anything else to lose at this point though, and he had been desperate to find a way to make this heist work.

This whole thing really is crazy, he thinks to himself, and she is crazy for suggesting it. Crazy, and wild. That thought leads him to a few other naughty, wild thoughts about the woman he loves, and he looks over at her, watching the river, her hair blowing in the wind, still fidgeting with the coffee cup in her hands, which is now empty.

Suddenly he's filled with this overwhelming feeling of love for her, and not just that, but he's turned on like mad by her crazy scheming mind, and seeing just how wild she could really be, that there are still depths to her he hasn't discovered yet. He reaches up and brushes some hair away from the base of her neck, making her shudder, just wanting to touch her. Hell, all this talk has gotten him so worked up that he almost wants to take her, right here on the embarkment to the river, right here out in the open, in view of the public. He just wants to be with her and be inside her.

Demi lets out a laugh, picking up on his vibe from the way that he's touching her, and the way that his breathing has picked up as he leans in closer to her, touching her hair. Plus, that boner he's sporting is something she could see a mile away, anyone could, and the thought makes her smirk.

She leans into him as well, looking upwards and kissing him lightly, teasingly, running her tongue ever so gently along his bottom lip, knowing he loves it. "Maybe we should go back to the hotel and get a little bit of rest before our big night," she says huskily, pulling his lip in between her teeth and nibbling on it gently.

Adam can't help but moan loudly at the thought, turned on even more so by her actions, and he reaches over and takes her hand and runs her palm along his thigh, up between his leg and over his rock-hard cock, desperately aching to be freed, pressed up against his pants. Showing her just how badly he wants her. She gives him a little squeeze on the sensitive head, right through his pants, and he does more than moan this time, gripping the back of her head with his hands and pulling her face close, kissing her deeply.

They kiss passionately for a few minutes, making out like horny teenagers, hands all over one another, before Adam finally breaks away, even though he's aching for more. "Let's go," he says, "I have things to do to you," taking her hand and getting up on his feet quickly, then pulling her up afterwards, pressing her up against him.

Now she can feel just how horny he is, so tight up against her, poking her, and they kiss a little longer standing by the river, lost in each other, before holding hands and making their way back to the hotel, eager to be with one another.

Chapter Sixteen

There is an odd tension that's growing and building between them as they prepare for the heist that afternoon. Part of it is sexual, but part of it is nervousness and excitement too, and an uncertainty of the unknown. They are both feeling such a wide mixture of emotions that it's almost hard to concentrate on any one thing, and they end up getting tense and snippy with each other when they don't mean to, simply feeling overwhelmed as the day goes on.

They have also gone over a hundred different scenarios and have talked out every single way the evening could possibly go, just as many times, and that has their nerves on edge as well. The first idea Demi suggested was that she show up there with an accidental delivery of some sorts, but Adam really laughed hard at that one and put a stop to her idea before it went any further.

"If you don't see how fake and cheesy that sounds, you're killing me," he says to her when he finally stops laughing. "This whole thing boarder lines on sounding like a porno movie in the first place, and we don't need to add to that. No. It needs to be far more authentic, real sounding, she needs to trust you right off the hop."

They talk a little while longer about different scenarios, but Adam doesn't really have any other suggestions other than he just doesn't want this to throw up any red flags for the wife. If they are going to do this, then he wants, needs, to make sure that they do this right.

Next, Demi suggests that they do some research on the house itself, and some more research on the couple, specifically around how long they have lived at that address, and where they came from before, and some information about the past owners. Maybe they could trigger something from that. A fake sales call or a pretend friend of a past house occupant.

Adam finds himself having another one of those moments where he is incredibly turned on by her mind, and the way she thinks and the way she is scheming behind the scenes and coming up with plans. She was a lot like him, and she was perfect for him. He finds himself falling more and more in love with her every day.

A few good old google internet searches provides them with all the information that they need to know; everything is on the internet these days, right at your fingertips. The jeweler and his wife had bought the house only seven years prior and had lived in another state before that. The owners before them had been house flippers, and had bought the house a year before *that*, done some renovations and sold it to the jeweler.

However, the people that owned the house before all of that had been a married couple with kids who would have been their age right now, Demi calculates after some quick math. She also checks the length of time that the family had owned the house and realizes that the kids would have grown up in the home, and then moved before becoming adults and moving out on their own. That's when she felt a new plan forming in her mind.

After a little more research, and after letting Adam have his way picking as many holes through the plan as possible so that they can work out all the kinks and every single detail, they decided on the following plan. Demi is going to play it off like she is the now grown up daughter of the very first occupants of the house, who Demi also looks up to make sure don't still live in this town and might actually be recognized by the wife. Luck seems to be on their side for this crazy plan so far, because that family had moved many states away when they sold the house to the house flippers and haven't left since.

They are going to hope that the gate will still be open like last night, betting on the fact that the wife is forgetful or just genuinely doesn't care, and Demi is going to use that to her advantage to walk right up to the front door and knock. If the gate is closed, she will work with it, but she has a good feeling that they are going to find that gate open when they get there tonight.

She plans to wait until after dinner, closer to bedtime, after the sun sets and it gets dark. Adam will drop her off a few blocks away and let her walk there, and he will drive around and then park back later down the street when it's pitch black. If anything goes wrong before that, like Demi not being able to get into the house, she can always call him to come and get her. Basically, Demi is just going to walk on up to that door, knock, play the hell out of her part and hope for the best. She has spent some time studying the blueprints of the house now, along with the original blueprints of the house and all the photographs, and she feels confident she knows it well already, without ever having stepped foot inside of it.

It isn't a spectacular plan, they can agree on that, but it is all they have to go on, and they don't have much else to lose. Demi is going to gush and beg and flirt her way inside, so excited to be back in the neighborhood unexpectedly and so thrilled to see the house she grew up in once more, if the wife doesn't mind, which she knows she won't. She figures once she gets inside, it will be show time, but she also isn't going to push her luck too far too fast. If she can get the wife to bring out some wine, she is going to get a little flirty, and see how that goes. Ideally, she's hoping the wife will be game to let her take her to bed for a few hours, and then Adam can get on with the heist and go about stealing the diamonds without pressure or worrying if he is going to be caught at any moment.

Realistically, Demi knows that there is a chance the woman could turn her down sexually too, and simply not be interested, and then she will have to settle for being a friendly distraction and work with that, but she's really hoping that won't be the case. Now that they are really doing this, she is excited, and horny as all hell at the idea of what awaits her later that evening. She just hopes that by the end of it, Adam will be ok with her, and happy with what she's done.

So here they are, prepping for this crazy night ahead of them, the tension growing between them in this hotel room that feels both suffocating and also way too large all at the same time. Adam is finding it harder and harder to concentrate on the plan at hand and what's going on around him, and he's snapped on Demi a few times for it, even though he hasn't meant to. He's not upset with her or the situation at all, in fact, it's the complete opposite. Adam cannot stop thinking about the thought of his girlfriend in bed with the jeweler's wife, taking advantage of her, the scene in his head so hot and sexy as it plays out.

He's never thought about her with another woman, in fact, it's not something that's come up in any relationship before in his life. He's torn between feeling a little bit of anxiety and stress over the thought of her being with someone else, and possibly finding something there with the wife, or, finding out something about herself that may affect their relationship in some way. He's never had a discussion with her about her sexual past like that before and doesn't know if this is something that's new for her, or something she's done a time or two, or more, before.

The other part of him is torn on the fact that thinking about her with another woman is one of the hottest things he's thought about in a long time. He doesn't even need to be there, doesn't want to be involved or have to see it happen, it's just the *idea* of her in bed with the wife, another woman, both of their soft, sweet bodies pressed up against one another, naked and horny, touching each other, making each other cum. That thought alone is enough to drive him absolutely crazy, and give him the strangest, stress and anxiety filled boner he has ever had in his whole life. He just wants to pin Demi up against the hotel room wall right now, and take her like there's no tomorrow, reminding her of their magic together, but it's the worst time for that, and he can't stop thinking about the other side of that either, and his insecurities over the whole thing start to eat away at him.

So, the tension continues to grow between them as Demi double checks their bags and does one last look around the hotel room, trying to make sure they are fully prepared and not missing anything they need. She isn't feeling many of the same emotions that Adam is feeling; she is confident in her sexuality, and in her feelings for Adam and their relationship, and she is also feeling pretty confident that she can turn on the charm enough to lure the wife into her bedroom. Demi's only real concerns are if this crazy, wild heist is actually going to come together smoothly and they'll get away with it, just like something out of a porno, and if Adam is actually ok with her doing this and being with a woman.

Because she's not on the same wave length as Adam, when she catches him looking at her a bit strangely out of the corner of her eye while she's almost ready, she mistakes it for him checking her out, and so she gives her butt a little shake at him and laughs, drawing him out of his thoughts. "If this sweet ass is what you are day dreaming about over there boy," she says with a wink, "You'll just have to wait until later. We are ready to roll, and you need to keep your eyes on the prize. Well, the other prize."

Her joke shakes his mood up a bit, and he gives her a laugh in return, and mentally gives his head a shake as well, trying to get with the program. They have a lot to do tonight and a lot at stake in front of them if they are going to pull this off right, and he's lucky that things have started working out in their favor, and for that he really has Demi to thank. He's also very lucky for her ideas and scheming mind, and the fact that she's even willing to go along with him and with this in the first place. The thought picks his spirits up a bit, and he says to her, "How did I ever get so lucky?"

"Well, you did kind of kidnap me, remember?" she says back to him with a smile, and stands over where he is sitting on the bed, straddling his legs, and leans down for a quick kiss. Adam reaches up and pulls her closer in and turns their quick kiss into a long one filled with need, passion, and love. Demi pulls away with a laugh, reminding him again that they don't have time for any monkey business, and she turns away and goes back over their things again, feeling a little neurotic at this point, but terrified they've forgotten something.

Demi has even gone over her outfit a dozen times, and changed just as many, being sure to pay attention to every single detail, right down to the fact that her bra and panties match, and are very sexy, but not too sexy and over the top. A little less porn girl and a little classier, here on a business trip but still want to feel good about myself.

Adam can't watch her go through everything again, for the hundredth time, driving him bananas, so he gets up from the bed and grabs his own bags, packed with everything he could possibly need for tonight and then some, and heads to the doorway, letting her know that he's all ready and that now, they're just waiting on her.

She laughs in somewhat annoyance, more so at herself for knowing that he's right, and she needs to get a move on, and she takes one last, long look around the place, herself and her bag, and then takes a deep breath and joins him at the doorway, ready to go. Instead of grabbing the door handle though, Adam reaches over and takes her by the back of the head gently, pulling her close, pulling her into him for one last kiss in the room, before they head out for the heist.

Chapter Seventeen

They stop to get a bite to eat on the way to the house. Neither of them are all that hungry, but they both know there is a long night ahead of them, and they need to be on their a-game, which includes eating. It's late for dinner, but that fits perfectly with their plan, and they both managed to force some food down. When they arrive on the planned street, it hasn't quite grown dark enough yet for Adam to drop Demi off. They want the wife to have had time to eat dinner herself, and relax and unwind a bit, before Demi shows up and tries to sweet talk her way into the house.

During the drive over here, Demi feels her emotions jumping all over the map, and slowly she begins to lose a little bit of that confidence she has been building up. Her thoughts are racing over time, imagining all sorts of what ifs and things that could go wrong, and she forces herself to breathe deep and calm her mind, and her wildly beating heart, and watch the city pass by out her window.

She's still feeling extremely excited about the whole thing; it's been a long time since she's been with a woman, and if she's being honest with herself, that sexual release is something she is definitely looking forward to experiencing again. It's not something she has done a lot in her life, but it's not new to her either; she does love the feel of a woman's soft body beside her, underneath her, and the taste and smell of a pussy is intoxicating to her.

She's also feeling very nervous about the heist as well though, and that feeling isn't sexual at all. There still are a lot of unknowns in this scenario, there is a lot of room for error, and for things to go wrong. They have been lucky so far in a lot of aspects, even so much as the way this plan has all come together, but they don't know for certain that it's even going to work, period, and never mind just by Demi being turned down at the door. They could get there tonight, and the wife could be entertaining a whole house full of people. It could be wine and bridge night with the girls. Maybe a friend will be coming by. Or maybe, the wife will end up bringing by a secret lover of her own. Maybe that's why they are having issues in their marriage and fighting and not taking trips together.

To top all of *that* off, she still doesn't quite know how Adam really feels about all this, and that has her feeling on edge itself. More so than anything else she's experiencing. She doesn't know if he's secretly into this, if he doesn't really care one way or another, or if he's sitting over there being eaten alive by insecurities about her being with another woman. They have just been so busy talking about all the plans, the what ifs, how they were going to actually pull this off, that they never really stopped to talk *to* each other, about what was happening, or how it was going to affect them, or how they each felt about it. And it is all happening so fast, suddenly they are parked down the street from the house, and Demi has been so lost in thought, she's missed the entire drive, only just snapping out of her thoughts now.

Adam planned for them to arrive a little bit early, on the other side of the street and further down the block, to have a once over of the house and a final go over of the plans before they went forward with it, but they are still earlier than that, and have time to kill. They want to make sure that the wife is going to be home, and alone, so that their plan can work. Once they know everything is a go, they will start the car again and leave, and Adam will drop Demi off a little further down the block, and it'll be go time.

Demi looks beautiful, but not too over the top or dramatic or fake either. She looks classy, and gorgeous as far as Adam is concerned, dressed as if she is here for some kind of corporate work event. She looks delicious, and he wishes he could show her just how good he thinks she looks. She plans to play it off like she hasn't been back in the area in years, and she was simply thinking about this place on the way back to her hotel and decided to swing by her old house on a whim. She'd had so many amazing memories growing up in that house, and desperately wanted to see it again.

She plans to be charming and friendly and just a touch flirty, playing off that she's just bored and very lonely, being back in the city without knowing anyone, and if she gets a good vibe from that and they start hitting it off, she's going to play it up like she'd really love to not sit all alone in her hotel room all night. From what they already know about the wife, this should go over well.

They have some time left before they have to go, and Adam uses the binoculars to check in on the wife a few times, to confirm everything is good. So far, everything seems very similar to the night before. The wife appears to be wandering back and forth throughout the house, doing some tidying up after a late dinner, and enjoying a glass of wine. They decide to give her a little bit more time, to let her get finished everything she needs to do and settle in with her night and relax, so that Demi doesn't interrupt anything the wife has going on and make her feel pressured to end the conversation at the doorway.

Timing is everything with this plan, and they both need to be on the ball. Once Demi gets inside the house, Adam is going to keep a close eye on everything from the outside, so that he'll know exactly when he can make his way inside and sneak into the office and pull off the heist while the wife is distracted.

As this runs through his head, Adam finds himself laughing out loud, and the sound is startling in the tense silence of the car. Demi can't possibly imagine what's so funny right now, but before she has a chance to ask him, he blurts out, "So, my cue to enter and pull off this heist is, realistically, when my girlfriend takes the wife of the guy we're robbing into the bedroom to have sex with her as a diversion, keeping her out of the way."

Demi is still staring out the window while he says this, and she inhales sharply and all but freezes, totally thrown off by his comment. She can't seem to read the tone of his voice and can't tell whether that was supposed to be a sexy comment, and something she was supposed to laugh at, or if he's feeling mad, jealous, or insecure about the whole thing, and if laughing is the last thing she's supposed to do. She's feeling so torn, and almost sick with worry now, that she says nothing at all, just keeps staring out the window and fidgeting with her hands, wondering if all of this was a bad idea.

Adam glances over at her, slightly caught off guard by her demeaner, wondering why she didn't even attempt a laugh at his lame joke. He can tell that something is off with her, but he doesn't know what it is, if it's the upcoming heist in general, if it's what she's supposed to do with the wife, or if it's him, or something else he hasn't even thought of yet. At this point, they are both on edge for all sorts of reasons.

He knows that neither of them are on their a-game right now either, too focused on what's going on inside their own heads, and that isn't how he wants this heist to start. If they're going to sit here for a little while longer, they need a distraction, and he knows the perfect one.

Demi is still looking out the window and doesn't see him when he reaches out for her. It takes her by surprise to feel his hand gently cup her chin and turn her face towards him. Adam leans in and pulls her close to him, kissing her passionately, urgently, his tongue snaking out and lightly trailing its way along her soft, almost trembling lips.

He can feel her entire body grow rigid beneath him, and she almost tries to pull away from him, but he is relentless, and has to have her, right here, right now, before any of this goes down tonight. His tongue pushes its way into her mouth, caressing hers, kissing her deeply, and he feels her sigh and moan into him. He doesn't let up, and his hands are all over her body, touching her everywhere, wanting all of her, every last inch of her, needing her.

She tries again to pull away from him, thinking about the task at hand that's about to start soon, and all of the stressful thoughts that are running through her head, but then she feels him pinching at her nipples through her shirt, and grabbing around her waist, and then one of his hands slips between her legs. Now she's moaning his name instead, and her attempts to get away from him are growing weaker and weaker, all of her stressful thoughts leaving her for the time being.

Adam can tell that she's starting to crack; he knew she would. The chemistry between them is unreal as it is, and he knows just how to turn her on, and how to touch her to make her feel good, to make her beg him for more. He uses this weakening opportunity to grab her around the waist and lift her up, pulling her onto his lap in the driver's seat. It's a tight fit, but they cram in there, her sitting on his lap, with one of his hands on the back of her neck, pulling her face into his, kissing all her protests away.

He keeps his other hand busy too, slowly trailing his fingertips along her thighs, and then tucking them underneath her skirt. He feels her body shake in anticipation, and her legs slowly part, giving him more access between her thighs, giving herself up to him. His fingers make their way over the top of her panties, pulling them open, and he slides his hand inside, feeling her shift once again to allow him room. Adam spreads her lips wide and rubs her swollen pussy, finding her soaking wet, and she moans loudly, pushing herself back against him, opening herself up for more. Demi no longer wants him to stop.

Her next moans are muffled by Adam's mouth as he leans in and kisses her, stifling her cries of passion. He's still holding onto the back of her head, fingers entwined in her hair, pulling her close. Her body is trembling on top of him, pulsating, begging for more.

The hand he's got tucked between her legs never stops. His fingers continue to slide up and down her slit, getting completely covered in her juices, before he parts her wet folds and pushes two of them inside of her tight hole. Demi cries out into his mouth, and he fingers her roughly, pushing them into her harder and harder, using his thumb to press against and rub her hard clit.

Demi's cries are getting difficult to stifle as she moans and gasps and trembles on his lap. He feels her hands on him, as she pulls him even closer to her, her nails digging into him in her urgency. And her hands aren't the only things clinging to him tightly; her pussy walls are milking his fingers, and her juices are leaking all down his hand.

Adam picks up speed, thrusting his fingers harder, and deeper, inside of her. He finally breaks their long, wet kiss, and slowly kisses along the edge of her lips to the side of her face, and then trails his tongue along her ear. Her entire body shudders against him, and this time her mouth is free to moan his name. He makes his way down to her neck and collar bone, kissing and nibbling on her tender skin, while he continues to finger her sweet hole.

Demi is moaning louder now, not far from an orgasm, and she grabs onto his shoulder and arm tightly, holding him against her, while she thrusts her hips against his hand, in time with his fingers. Adam just keeps pushing them in and out of her, and he pulls her face back close to his and once more muffles her cries with a deep, wet kiss. The feel of his tongue on hers, in time with his fingers inside of her, is enough to set her over the edge, and she moans into his mouth, digging her fingertips into him as she pulls him closer, a hard orgasm gripping her.

Adam holds her close as she cums, her pussy pulsing tightly around his fingers, her body vibrating in his lap. He breaks their kiss and pulls his lips away from hers, allowing her to catch her breath, but he keeps kissing her everywhere else, her cheeks, ear, neck, and chin, as she comes down from her orgasm, loving the taste of her skin.

Once she's had a chance to calm down, he slowly slides his hand out from between her legs and adjusts her underwear and skirt for her. Then he pulls her even closer into him, still sitting in the cramped drivers seat, now feeling even more tight since they're no longer lost in the heat of the moment. Plus, now that Demi is a little more in the here and now, she can feel something long and hard poking into her ass from underneath her.

She lets out a little laugh, feeling almost giddy, having forgotten all the stress and anxiety of what lies ahead for a little while, and she snuggles her body tightly against his, pressing her ass up against his hard cock, slowly grinding herself along the length of it. "I hope that helped you relax a little bit, you were feeling so tight and tense," Adam says with a laugh himself, feeling a bit nervous, nuzzling his face into her neck.

They spend a few more minutes like that, tightly wrapped up in each other's arms, neither one of them wanting to be the first to admit that time is running out, and that they have to get a move on soon. Adam still has a rock-hard cock; between the thought of what's coming with Demi and the wife, the hot scene that just transpired between them, and the fact that Demi is still sitting on him, her ass hot against his aching member, his hard on isn't going anywhere.

"Mmm, there will be more of this later," she says with a moan, thrusting her hips up and down on him a few times and kissing the corner of his mouth. "And there better be a story to go with it," Adam says with a growl, and pushes himself up into her, poking her, wishing he was burying his dick inside of her right now, wanting to pin her down in the backseat.

They kiss and cuddle for a few more minutes, but the time has come, and shortly afterwards Demi climbs off Adam and back into the passenger seat. She takes a few minutes to make sure that she is back to looking pretty and presentable, and she fixes her clothes and hair and make-up especially, making sure she doesn't have that "freshly fucked" look.

When Demi is ready and feeling confident, as much as she can be, Adam starts the car, and they drive off towards the next street over, where Adam plans to drop her off.

Chapter Eighteen

Demi gets out of the car on shaky legs, feeling nervous, excited, and unsure of herself, all at the same time. She forces in a deep breath, steadying herself, and then she takes one last look back into the car, and sees Adam blowing her a kiss. She lets out a small laugh, and catches it, amused by his cheesy gesture, and feeling a little better because of it. Then she shuts the door, and suddenly he's gone; driving off and leaving her standing there on the sidewalk.

She knows that he isn't going far, simply driving around the block to the other side of the house, and parking on another street, where he will be able to watch the entire thing from the car and wait for his cues. However, right now in the moment, she feels incredibly alone.

She still doesn't know what came over her either, or where this crazy plan had even come from in the first place. Everything just happened so fast, and now here she is, heading towards the house, about to seduce the wife so her boyfriend could rob this woman's husband, a heist they had originally planned to do together, in what was supposed to be an empty house. And while she may have been with women before in her past, she has never done *anything* quite like this before; seducing an unsuspecting total stranger, and a married woman at that! She doesn't even know if the wife is going to find her attractive or will actually want to cheat on her husband. Just because she seems unhappy, doesn't mean Demi can assume anything else.

And yet here she is, getting closer and closer to the house, forcing her feet to slow down so they don't take her there before she's ready. Demi is still feeling nervous and knows that won't do; she needs to get herself into the part she's supposed to be, and feeling confident about it, if they're going to pull this off and make it work. And they need to make it work.

She has the person she's supposed to be memorized fairly well, dates, birthdays, family members, whereabouts, any other information she'd been able to find that might come in handy, as well as dates of when that family would have moved, etc. Adam thinks she's a bit neurotic, and that's not the first time that's been thrown around, but Demi wants to take this seriously. She doesn't know what information she might need in the moment, and she wants to have it all. She'd also gone over dozens of floor plans and photographs of the home, especially those done before the renovations, just in case, so she knew the original house by memory.

Demi takes a few slow, deep breaths, settling her racing heart, and her racing mind, as she draws closer and closer to the house. She knows Adam can probably see her by now, although she doesn't look for the car, not wanting to make anything obvious. Instead, she starts taking in everything else around her, as if she hasn't been back to this place in almost two decades. She already knows how she plans to establish a solid conversation and a foundation of trust off the hop, by mentioning some key heartfelt things about growing up here like the tree that used to hold her old tire swing, and changes to the outside property where she used to play.

Going over the plan in her head again, and solidifying what she is doing here once more, helps calm her a bit, and she takes a few more deep breaths, approaching the front of the property. She is relieved to see that the gate is still open like last night, and she can just walk right up to the house and knock, without having to deal with the locked gate. So far, so good.

The courtyard leading up to the house is already fairly lit up, with small outdoor bulb lights tucked among the gardens and along the stone edges of the walkways, but as she approaches the house she sets off the motion detector lights that she didn't know were there, and the whole front walkway lights up in daylight.

Her heart catches in her throat, startled, being unexpectedly caught in the spotlight. The lights must have been turned off when they were creeping around so late last night, she thinks, because they never set them off, and now she's almost frozen in spot, not realizing there was a motion detector set up, and kicking herself for not knowing. Yet she unclenches her fists from her sides and keeps walking to the front door, determined not to falter. She's not the one coming here to sneak around tonight, she's coming to knock on the door and hopefully be let in to see her childhood home, so the lights shouldn't matter to her.

When she reaches the door and goes to knock, she realizes her breath is still racing and her heart is still hammering, and her emotions are all over the map, so she forces herself to slow down for a minute and focus everything she's got on the task at hand. You got this, you sexy bitch, she says to herself in her head, taking one more long, slow deep breath, and then she knocks loudly on the front door.

It takes a few minutes for the wife to answer the door, and while she waits, Demi finds herself shifting back and forth from foot to foot with anxiety. She goes to stop herself, and then doesn't. Regardless of who she is right now, or who she's supposed to be, she is still a stranger, showing up at a stranger's house at night, and so she should be allowed to be a little bit nervous. It is a strange request, to show up unannounced to your childhood home, while maybe not totally unheard of, and she wonders again if she's going to be able to convince this lady to let her in, and if they're going to be able to pull off this heist, or if this whole plan really is crazy, and a bust in the making.

Suddenly, the door opens, and the wife is standing right there in front of her, and this is really happening. Her breath catches in her throat, and Demi feels like someone pulled the ground out from under her, everything starts spinning.

"Hello?" The wife says questioningly, but she doesn't look all that concerned or alarmed. That's a good start, Demi thinks, forcing herself to get with it. "Hi!" Demi says back cheerfully, putting on a big smile. She wastes no time jumping right into character and even though she can't help but talk fast anyway, she still lets herself speed through, knowing that her fast talk will actually help add to her excitement of being back here, and possibly help skip over any lingering details that she may have missed as she goes.

Demi starts by introducing herself with the name of the person she's pretending to be and tells the woman that she's a former tenant of the house. "I grew up here," she says to the wife in the doorway, "And it has been many, many years since I've ever been back here. In fact, I don't think I've ever been back here in my adult life. I just happened to have to come to the city for a business event, and then it ran kind of late. I was taking a cab back to my hotel, and ended up driving past the neighborhood, and I got to thinking about this house, then on a whim I asked the cab driver to drop me off, but I took the number, so I could call another cab after. I just, uh, really had to come back here again, walk through the neighborhood, see all the changes. What you have done with the place is beautiful too by the way, oh my goodness. And the tree is still there that held my old tire swing. It's just, I don't know anyone in the city anymore, and I'm all alone here for the night and really didn't want to go straight back to my hotel, I just wanted to see this place again while I was in the area, just to kill some time. I'm so sorry. And oh, my goodness here I am just rambling away, telling you my whole life story, please, forgive me, I'm so embarrassed."

Demi lets out a cute laugh at this, knowing damn well she isn't rambling at all, hoping that this overwhelming amount of information, and all her rehearsed backstory, is going to help win this woman over and help get her into the house.

The wife laughs, but it's a friendly laugh. "Oh, this is too funny! Wow. How nice it is that you grew up here! No, I really don't mind at all that you've stopped by unannounced, don't even worry about it." Demi sees this as an opening, and so she continues with her spiel. "The gardens here are gorgeous, did you put them in yourself? My mother was never much of a gardener. And the pond, oh my goodness! You really have just made this place look amazing. Again, I'm so sorry for barging over so late like this, seriously. I hope I'm not interrupting anything."

Once again, the wife laughs, but this time she steps back from the door slightly and introduces herself. "I'm Amber, by the way. It's nice to meet you, fellow house liver. I'm actually not busy at all, and I'd love some company. Would you like to come in? You can check out some of the other renovations that have gone on in the house, and see everything that we've done with the place?"

It's as if a genie has sprung forth and granted Demi the first of her three wishes. Poof. It was that easy. She has to stop herself from laughing out loud at the thought. That won't do. Besides, she knows that the hard part has only just begun. Now she needs to actually keep up the charade, seduce this woman, take her to the bedroom and keep her there and distracted long enough for Adam to rob the husband's office of all the jewels and money. Her job has only started.

Demi steps inside the doorway after Amber, and the wife shuts the door behind them. Instantly, Demi is hit with a lovely fragrance of flowers, and the warm air of the house is a nice contrast from the cool air outside. She follows the wife down the hallway, and Amber leads the way into the kitchen. The house is breathtaking inside, and Demi looks around slowly, trying to take it all in and compare it to the pictures she's tucked in her head as she goes.

There is music playing softly in the living room, and in the kitchen there is a half drank glass of wine on the counter. Amber asks her if she would like a glass, and Demi gratefully agrees, thinking to herself once again that this part has been so very easy. Now, she's wondering if there's going to be a catch afterwards, and how bad it's going to be.

They stand there for a little while talking in the kitchen. Not so much about the house now, but more so about each other, getting to know one another a little bit now that Amber has let her into her home. And Amber is quick and eager to open up to Demi, telling her that her husband is away on business, and that she had wanted to go, and was supposed to, but he hadn't wanted her to and cancelled on her at the last minute. They were having problems, again, and things were really unhappy between them right now. And she didn't have many friends or get out much either, and didn't really have anyone to talk to, which is why she was home alone drinking wine when Demi showed up.

Now it is Amber's turn to apologize for rambling, but Demi doesn't mind at all. She genuinely feels for this woman, and is actually glad that somehow, this is how it's all turned out. She's really enjoying sharing some wine with her and chatting in the kitchen, and getting to know her, as crazy as that all is.

Amber offers to pour them both another glass of wine, and Demi accepts whole heartedly. They continue talking, and now they make their way from the kitchen into the living room, and Amber leads them to the big bay windows overlooking the backyard. From here, Demi can see more of the ponds and the gardens, and the tree that she and Adam used to gain access to the yard without being seen. Demi mentions the gardens again, and how beautiful they are, realizing now that Amber can talk forever about flowers and gardening, and anything that keeps this going and helps develop things further between them is great.

Since she's spoke about growing up here a few times, Demi takes the opportunity to make a few comments about different places and spots in the house, memories, siblings, what it was like here, establishing some more trust. Now that there is a bit of wine flowing through her, she finds the conversation is easy, and she's fallen into character quite nicely.

At the mention of her siblings, Amber offers to give Demi a tour of the rest of the house, so she can see what they have done with all of the other renovations. Bingo, Demi thinks to herself with a smirk, and then gushes excitedly about being able to see her old bedroom once again, the room that she grew up in, where she has the most memories.

They make their way down the hallway, and Demi almost pushes Amber out of the way in "eagerness", mentally thanking herself for being so anal about going over the floor plans to the house, because even though she's never been here before, she feels she knows the place well, so well she could make her way around it blindfolded. She bursts through the doorway, finding the spare room that they had watched

Amber from the night before, and Demi all but throws herself down on the bed, laughing in excitement.

"I'm sorry, it's just so crazy and exciting to be back here," Demi laughs with a slightly embarrassed laugh, but Amber doesn't hesitate and takes a seat beside her on the bed and joins her in the laughter, the feeling contagious.

The two of them giggle on the bed for a few moments, giddy from the wine they've been drinking and lost in the fun of it all, when their eyes lock, and for just a second, there is something there between them. Instantly, Demi is certain of two things. One, it's not quite time yet, but Amber wants her. And two, this is actually going to fucking work.

The thought of that has her feeling even more giddy than she is already, if that's even possible, and she toasts her empty glass at Amber. "To new friends," she says with a wink. Amber toasts her back and proclaims, "New friends who need new wine," and the two of them get back up, giggling to each other, and they make their way back to the kitchen for more wine, arms linked, feeling like old high school friends now, rather than two strangers, with one lying simply to seduce the other in order to steal from her.

When they get back to the kitchen for a refill on wine, they get to talking again, leaning up close to one another against the counter, and Demi slowly begins to turn the charm on once more. A little bit heavier this time. She wonders if Adam is still in the car, or if he has made it into the backyard yet, and is possibly right outside the windows, waiting for his cue, watching her flirt with the wife, drinking and giggling.

The thought turns her on, and then the feeling is amplified when Ambers arm brushes her own; whether intentional or accidently, Demi doesn't know, and it doesn't matter. Their touch sends shocks through her, electrifying her skin, and she can't wait for more. She starts to dial up the charm a bit more, watching for cues from Amber, and always flirting back anytime Amber starts getting flirty. And she definitely is; the more she opens up to Demi, and gets comfortable with her, the flirtier she becomes. Demi is starting to wonder if she isn't the only one who switches teams from time to time and wonders how much easier Amber is going to make this for her tonight.

Suddenly they are on their second, or maybe their third glass of wine since they've returned to the kitchen, and Demi has no idea how much time has been passing, but she knows that she doesn't have all night. Adam is out there somewhere, waiting, watching, and the thought is giving her thrills again. The girls are openly flirting in the kitchen now, arms and hands touching frequently, and Demi knows this is not part of the plan. She has to get the wife out of here, and up into the bedroom, before they get on with their kinky business, so that Adam can get on with his.

Grabbing her glass of wine, Demi declares in a mocking, drill Sargent type tone, "Onward, solider, there is still more of the house I've yet to see." Amber laughs hard at this, and taking her own glass of wine in hand, they make their way throughout the rest of the house.

Walking down the hallway, they pass a closed door, of which behind lies the office that contains everything Adam plans to rob later. "This was my brothers room," Demi says, tapping on the door slightly, pretending to feel nostalgic. "That's my husband's office now," Amber says with a sullen tone. "He hates it when I go in there, except to clean." "Hmm, isn't that funny," Demi replies, "My brother was the same way with my mother and I. Men."

The two ladies share a laugh in the hallway, holding each other's arms, and another moment passes between them. Demi can't help wondering again if Adam is watching them, and if he's getting as turned on by what's going on as she is. Demi knows that realistically, at this point, they have both had enough to drink that she could probably just keep the wife in the living room or kitchen and get her talking, and distract her that way, but she wants more. She wants to go all the way through with this, and have her sweet way with the wife, and taste her juicy pussy. She can almost smell it, so close against her in the hallway.

Besides, Amber has not been shutting Demi's advances down, and she's had plenty of opportunity to do so. Instead, she's damn near dragging Demi down the hallway now, right to the very place in the house Demi wants them to be. The Master Bedroom.

Demi follows Amber into the bedroom, taking in everything around her. It's very neat, clean and well kept, and clearly, neither of the married pair spend much time in here. There is an adjacent bathroom, and that's what Demi hears Amber talking about now, as she comes out of her thoughts and back into reality.

"We did an entire gut of the ensuite bathroom when we moved in. I wasn't sure about the bathtub, so I got rid of it and put in this gorgeous jacuzzi and the stand-up shower over there. Plus, we added that extra window for more light. I just love it." Amber tells her. "I never did spend a whole lot of time in here," Demi replies, looking around and pretending to take in all of the changes, "As it was my parents private bathroom, but I did come in here from time to time, and what you've done with the place looks beautiful. I absolutely love it."

Demi does a little circle in the bathroom, taking everything in around her, and when she spins around once more, Amber is standing right there, so close to her that they are almost touching again. Hmm, Demi thinks to herself, and who is supposed to be seducing who over here.

The two of them are standing by the bathroom counter, and Demi can see both of their reflections in the mirror. She takes a half a step forward, placing her glass of wine on the counter, leaving both of her hands free, and Amber does the same, setting her own glass down and then takes one step closer to Demi. Now they are standing inches from one another, staring into each other's eyes, and that spark, that connection is back, only now, it's magnified tenfold. Demi can't wait to see how high it can get.

She leans in, closing the distance between them, and presses her soft, smooth lips against Amber's own slightly trembling ones. Amber feels a touch of hesitation, but only for a second, and then she is kissing Demi back with even more passion, and urgency, then Demi had kissed her. They both taste like wine, and as Demi pushes her tongue between Amber's lips, and feels her moan into her mouth, Demi remembers that someone may very well be watching them. She moans back, and then the two of them are all over each other in front of the bathroom mirror, eager for more.

"I don't even understand how this is happening," Amber says with a laugh between kisses, "Where did you ever come from tonight?" "Oh, you know," Demi says, kissing along her neck, feeling Amber push her curvy body up against her own, "I just came by on a whim for a hopeful tour of the house. But I will gladly take a tour of you in the bedroom as well." She feels Amber tremble at her words, and moan into her mouth once more, kissing her again urgently, and the two slowly make their way back into the bedroom.

Chapter Nineteen

Demi's head is spinning, and it has nothing to do with the wine she's been drinking. Her thoughts are all over the place, from how unbelievably easy all of this has turned out to be so far, to how horny she is right now. All she can think about, all she wants to do, is rip all of Amber's clothes off, tie her to the bed, and ravish her and make her feel good, and loved, and to make her cum over, and over, and over again, and to have Amber make Demi cum as well. She isn't even thinking about the heist anymore, sex is the only thing on her mind.

She doesn't want to press her luck though, or scare this poor woman away, so she forces herself to calm down a bit and she lets Amber take the lead, especially as they've been drinking. She was all about seducing this girl, but in the end, she only wants Amber to do what she wants to do, and to take this as far as Amber wants it to go.

As far as the heist goes, Demi is finding it harder and harder to focus on that, the closer her and Amber get to each other. She is intoxicated with the wife, and has to have her, anyway she can have her. Adam could already be in the house by now, hell, for all she knows, he could be robbing the jewelry right now, or already done, and that still wouldn't stop her, she just wants to make love to Amber.

Now that they are in the bedroom, having made their way over beside the bed, the girls stand close together once more, feeling giggling and flirty, and a little bit hesitant. Both of them thinking about what's to come now that they are really here in the bedroom, and if they are truly going to go forward with this. Amber reaches out for Demi slowly, and Demi steps into her arms, cupping the back of Amber's own head with her hands and bringing their faces close together.

They kiss again, and fireworks explode once more, as their tongues rub against each other, lips parting, exploring each other's soft wet mouths. Amber moans into her, and Demi presses her hips against Amber's, showing her that she is just as turned on, that she wants this just as much, she needs her just as badly.

Demi runs her hands along Amber's arms again, pulling her in closer, and Amber mimic's her movements, her hands and fingers so soft on Demi's skin. Amber's hands don't stop; feeling bolder now, they trail up along Demi's arms, over her shoulders, along the sensitive skin of her neck, and then she buries them in Demi's hair, as Demi had done to her a moment earlier.

Suddenly, any reservations Amber may have still had lingering seem to vanish now that she has Demi in her arms. She starts to kiss Demi deeper, harder, pushing her tongue against her own, her tongue soft and gentle, yet firm and needy. Their bodies are grinding against each other, eager for one another's touch. Amber slides her hands back down Demi's back, and then they slip underneath her shirt, her hands so soft and gentle, touching so lightly, teasing on her skin.

That's all the invitation Demi needs to go further with this, and she slides her hands underneath Amber's shirt too, feeling her smooth, taunt skin under her palms, running her hands up her spine, over her bra strap, and along her shoulders. The two of them make out this way for a little while, soft, gentle, wet, needy, exploring each other's bodies with their hands, while they explore each other's mouths with their tongues. Both growing hotter, wanting more, needing release.

It seems like both of their knees grow weak at the same time, and they tumble onto the bed that they're standing beside, sprawling out across the covers. They kiss a few more times, slowly, sensually, rolling around on the bed and grinding their bodies up against one another. Demi begins kissing down Amber's neck, and along her collar bone, and she feels Amber sigh and almost melt into her, all the tension escaping from her body.

"My husband never touches me like this," Amber says in a sigh, running her hands up Demi's soft stomach, feeling brave and cupping one of her breasts through her bra. "In fact, he never touches me at all. I'm not convinced he's not cheating on me, and I don't even care anymore. I just wish he would have touched me like *this* once in a while, because this feels so good."

Demi pushes her chest into Amber's hand, loving the feel of Amber's small palms on her breasts, wanting more, wanting to feel her bare skin. She reaches up under Amber's shirt with her own hand, and pushes Amber's bra aside, and pinches one of Amber's nipples. "A woman is supposed to feel good, and loved, and wanted," she says, kissing her way down Amber's neck, and then pulling her shirt up and over her head, exposing her, "And tonight I want to make you feel exactly that."

Amber moans as she helps Demi undress her, wiggling out of her t-shirt entirely, and then letting Demi unclasp and remove her bra. She lay there topless on the bed in front of Demi, and Demi takes her all in, loving the sight of her. She leans down and begins kissing along Amber's collar bone again, this time on the underside, and her hand returns to its exploration of her breasts and nipples.

As Demi kisses closer and closer to Amber's chest, Amber begins pushing herself off the bed, eager for more. "Mmm," she moans, withering under Demi, anxious for her mouth, wanting to feel Demi's gentle tongue on her. As Demi's soft lips move downwards still, Amber feels them lightly trace across one of her nipples, Demi's hot breath contrasting on her tight, cool skin, and she cries out when she feels Demi's hot tongue circle around one before sucking it lightly into her mouth.

"Oh my god, *no one* has ever touched me like this," Amber all but growls, and she reaches down and runs her fingers through Demi's hair, loving the silky feel of it beneath her fingers. "Please, more," she gasps, as Demi's other hand finds her other breast and begins to pull and tweak on that nipple, while still sucking and tonguing on the other one, "Make me cum."

Demi can't help but laugh slightly into Amber's chest at her eagerness, and her giggle sends vibrations through Amber's nipple, making her cry out again. "Oh, you're going to cum alright," Demi promises in a whisper, and continues licking and kissing along Amber's nipple, then slowly trailing her way over to the other one, feeling it harden in her mouth too.

Amber's skin is so smooth, so soft, under Demi's touch, and she smells amazing; like sweet perfume and flowers, and Demi can't get enough of her, wanting to touch her, feel her, taste her, absolutely everywhere she can.

Slowly, she makes her way down Amber's delicious body, kissing her way gently between her breasts, and down across her tight stomach. She reaches down and starts unbuckling Amber's pants, and Amber has no problem helping, thrusting her hips upwards to slide them down, and soon she's totally naked on the bed, with Demi sitting over her.

Eagerly Demi crawls between her legs, and Amber parts them, nervously, but wanting everything Demi will give her. Demi goes back to kissing her stomach, her hands lightly running along Amber's sides, pulling her close, feeling her body trembling below her as Amber moans and wiggles on the bed, anxious for more.

Using her hands first, she makes her way between Amber's thighs, parting them, and getting comfortable on the bed. Demi uses two of her fingers to spread her soft folds, and she feels Amber gasp loudly above her, reaching up and grabbing onto the sheets around her in anticipation of what's to come. With her other hand, Demi gently reaches out and touches Amber's exposed clit, ever so softly, rubbing her finger around it in circles as Amber cries out loud and almost arches herself off the bed, feeling electrified by Demi's touch.

Demi teases her like this for a few minutes before slowly sliding her fingers down and slipping one, and then two of them, inside Amber's tight hole. "Oooh, yesssss," Amber moans, pushing her hips downwards onto Demi's hand, her fingers disappearing deep inside.

Her pussy is so tight, almost clinging to Demi's fingers as she slowly begins to finger fuck Amber's wet hole, watching it swallow her fingers, eager for more. Demi lets out a moan herself, so turned on at the sight on the bed before her, and she leans forward and ever so slowly, takes Amber's hard clit into her mouth, rubbing it with her lips, and running her tongue along it, tasting her.

Amber is clutching the sheets around her now, bucking underneath Demi, all but throwing herself up off the bed into Demi, eager for more. One of her hands makes its way back down to Demi's head, and she entwines it in her hair, pulling her face in for more. Demi is happy to oblige, eagerly lapping and licking at Amber's clit and her soft wet folds as her fingers continue to push deep in and out of her tight hole.

Demi can tell it won't take Amber long to cum like this. Between all these new feelings and knowing just how soft and gentle a woman can be, this woman is going to cum all over her fingers and in her mouth very soon, and Demi can't wait to taste every drop. Amber's breathing picks up, and she is wiggling around on the bed, her slender, soft legs sliding up and down along Demi, pulling her close, wanting more.

Amber begins to gasp and moan, begging Demi to make her cum, digging her fingers into the top of her head, pulling Demi's mouth closer to her. Demi is happy to give her what she's asking for, licking her everywhere, pushing her fingers deep inside Amber, moving them around, touching all her sweet spots, sucking her hard, little clit between her soft lips.

All these sensations are too much for Amber and she cries out loudly, her thighs gripping Demi's shoulders tightly, hands pinning Demi's head close, her orgasm overtaking her. Demi feels Amber's sweet pussy walls tighten around her, and her tasty juices begin to drip down around Demi's fingers, and she laps it all up eagerly, not wanting to miss a drop.

Demi continues to lick and suck along Amber's soft folds and hard clit for a few more minutes, listening to her little mews as she comes down from her orgasm. Slowly, she pulls away, and as she sits upwards, suddenly Amber is on her, kissing her, laughing into her mouth as she draws Demi close to her. "That was incredible," she says breathlessly against Demi's lips, "And I can taste myself on your lips, which is so hot. Let me taste you now, it's my turn."

Demi laughs at Amber's eagerness, but she willingly agrees, anxious to feel Amber's soft gentle lips explore her somewhere else other than her mouth. She strips her top off, and then her skirt, leaving herself in just her matching underwear and bra, and she lays down on the bed beside Amber, inviting her to touch her, taste her, whatever and wherever she'd like.

Still naked, Amber sits beside Demi on the bed, and leans down and kisses her again, slowly this time, using more tongue, as she gets comfortable being in control. She lets her hands start to explore her body, feeling Demi's soft skin underneath her palms, feeling her skin break out into goosebumps at her gentle teasing touches. Demi moans, and Amber watches her face, enjoying knowing she's the one causing this pleasure.

Feeling bolder now, Amber makes her way down beside Demi's legs, so that she's leaning over her, with full view of her new lover. Demi sees her watching and stretches her arms up above her head, putting her body on display, giving herself a little wiggle and giggling, showing off. She slides her panties down, opens her legs a little more, and Amber can smell her, and see her tight little pussy lips, covered in juices. "Now it's your turn to make me cum," Demi whispers sexily.

Demi is clad now in only her bra, and Amber leans down, grabbing Demi's chest in her hands and pushing upwards, exposing her breasts from the top of her bra. Then she leans down further still and rubs her lips lightly over them both, one at a time, listening to Demi moan beneath her. She slowly takes one nipple into her mouth, licking and sucking on it gently, while she begins pinching and tweaking the other one, the same way she likes hers played with. Now Demi is withering around on the bed, anxious for more.

Amber makes her way other to Demi's other breast, now paying this one the same attention she gave the other one, feeling this one grow hard in her mouth too. Demi's slender body is pressing up against hers, pulling her close, and Amber knows she can't wait to feel her mouth and tongue down below. The thought of tasting a pussy for the first-time turns her on all over again.

Slowly, ever so slowly, Amber gets between Demi's legs and kisses her way down Demi's body, between her breasts, along the underside of her bra, and across her soft, smooth stomach. As she makes her way down, she runs her hands along Demi's sides, and the sides of her thighs, taking in every inch of her, not able to get enough of the feeling of her soft skin. She reaches Demi's belly button and slowly runs her tongue inside of it, feeling Demi jump and giggle underneath her. She loves having control over her like this and making her feel good.

Finally, Amber makes her way down between Demi's legs, and hesitantly she kisses along her pubic mound gently, little teasing kisses, driving Demi crazy underneath her. The smell and the sensations are driving Amber crazy as well, and she can't believe she's doing this. She keeps kissing Demi's skin, using her tongue to trail along lightly, and Demi is all but bucking herself up off of the bed to meet Amber's soft mouth.

"Oh, my goodness woman, you are driving me fucking mad," Demi says with a gasp, "Stop teasing me already!" Amber laughs, her mouth just on the soft skin above Demi's aching vagina lips, and this time its her laugh that sends vibrations coursing through Demi's entire body, making her moan loudly. Amber doesn't know where it's coming from but having all this sexual power over Demi is turning Amber on like she's never been before, and she can't wait to actually make Demi cum with her fingers, and her mouth, and taste her.

Amber reaches up between Demi's legs and ever so slowly, touches Demi's swollen pussy lips, rubbing them gently, up and down, before parting them, and getting a really good look at the scene in front of her. Demi all but squeals on the bed, loving being exposed like this, and loving Amber's slow hesitancy as she explores her, driving Demi wild, making her want to the climb the walls.

Then, finally, Amber leans forward and ever so slowly, she licks up the length of her slit, from Demi's tight hole to her hard, aching nub, tasting her for the first time. Both of them moan together, and then Amber can't stop herself, she has to taste her everywhere. She starts at the top at Demi's clit, slowly rubbing her lips around it and taking it into her mouth, gently sucking on it, doing to Demi what she knows she likes done to herself. When Demi moans in enjoyment, she runs her tongue around it a few times in circles, then alternates between the two.

Meanwhile, feeling a bit bolder still, she slides her fingers around Demi's soft folds a few times before finding her hole, and she pushes her middle finger against the tight opening, exploring Demi's pussy. "Yes, please," Demi begs, thrusting her hips upwards again, and Amber happily does as she's asked, and slowly, ever so slowly, she slides her finger inside.

She pulls away from Demi's clit and watches her finger slowly slide all the way in, and then out, and then back inside of Demi's folds. She is so silky and wet inside, and tight, and it's almost as if it's swallowing her finger ever time. She adds her first finger in with it, and Demi moans loudly, thrusting her hips upwards again to meet Amber's hand, her fingers disappearing inside once more.

"Oh, baby, please don't stop licking me at the same time, you're going to make me cum," Demi pants, thrusting her hips upwards again, clinging to the sheets around her, desperate for more, desperate for Amber's soft, gentle tongue all over her wet spots.

Amber waits just a few more teasing moments, watching her fingers hungerly be swallowed by Demi's swollen pussy lips, before leaning back down again and giving Demi exactly what she's begging and pleading for.

This time, there is no hesitancy in Amber's touch. Her mouth finds Demi's clit with ease, and she sucks that little, hard nub into her mouth, twirling it around her tongue. At the same time, she keeps pushing her fingers in and out of Demi, loving the feeling of her sweet tight pussy clenching around them. Demi's moans get louder and louder, and soon she is all but crying out for Amber, pushing herself off the bed, thrusting her hips into Amber's soft, sensual mouth, wanting it all.

By the way Demi is breathing, and moaning, and squirming all over the bed, Amber can tell she's about to make a woman orgasm for the first time in her life, and the thought sends thrills through her. Her fingers pick up speed, and her tongue and lips lick everywhere, from Demi's clit, along her lips and all her soft folds, joining her fingers, tasting all of Demi's juices as they leak out.

"Yes, oh yes," Demi cries out, clutching at the sheets, and she lets herself go as an orgasm takes her over the edge. Amber keep licking her, wiggling her fingers around deep inside, letting Demi ride out her orgasm, enjoying every drop of it. She keeps licking for so long that Demi has to stop her with a gasp, panting, holding onto her shoulders to all but pull her face away from between her legs, feeling far too sensitive at the moment.

"Holy shit Amber, that was incredible, are you sure you've never done that before?" Demi asks, laughing. "Now come back up here and hold me while I come down from that awesome orgasm." Amber laughs too, and crawls back up on the bed, joining Demi on the pillows. The two of them lay cuddled up for a few minutes, kissing and touching each other gently, their soft skin and smooth legs all over each other.

Then Amber sighs, smiling contently, and lays back on the bed, taking a deep breath. "Yeah, you're right, that was incredible," she says with another happy sigh. "I could have done that all night." "Oh," Demi says, sitting up on one elbow, looking Amber in the eyes, "Don't think that I'm done with you yet, beautiful. There is more fun to be had tonight."

Amber looks at her questioningly, but Demi doesn't say anything. Instead, she gets up, and slowly makes her way around the room, looking for something. Demi knows she may not even need to do this anymore; she doesn't know for sure, but the likely hood is that Adam is at least in the house right now getting everything out of the office, if not finished up by now. They have been in this bedroom for quite some time, and her job here is probably done.

Except, Demi isn't done. She isn't ready to leave, not with this beautiful woman in the bed beside her, eager for more. Demi wants more. She knows when she leaves this room, she is never going to see this woman again, and she's going to make it worth it, for both of them. Demi plans to take advantage of every single opportunity tonight.

She reaches the master bedroom closet, and opens it up, taking a look at what's inside. She hears Amber giggle on the bed behind her and ask her what she's searching for. Demi doesn't answer her at first, instead she reaches inside and takes out one of the husband's ties, and then she shuts the closet door again. She tosses the tie on the bed beside Amber, and says with a giggle, "Well, I found half of what I was looking for. Do you have any lube?" And finishes that off with a wink.

Amber laughs hard at that. "Yeah, there is some in my husband's nightstand. But what in the world do you need to lube up a tie for?" Now it's Demi's turn to laugh, and she's still laughing as she grabs the lube and crawls back into bed beside Amber, setting it down on the bed beside the tie. "Oh, sweetheart, you have a whole lot to learn about fun in the bedroom," she says.

She leans in and kisses Amber again, slowly, letting their lips part naturally and their tongues find each other again. Amber's body responds to hers so eagerly now, and Demi can't wait to explore her further. Demi runs her hands all over Amber's body once more, taking her all in, feeling her curves, her soft stomach, round breasts, hard nipples, pinching them slightly, feeling Amber shudder and moan beneath her again.

Demi trails her fingertips along the top of Amber's breasts, and then along her collar bone, over her shoulder, and then slowly makes her way up one of Amber's arms to her wrist, gripping it tightly, but not too tightly. She reaches for the tie, still kissing Amber deeply, and she feels Amber smirk into her mouth, and then break their kiss. "What are you up to?" She whispers.

"Don't worry," Demi whispers back, kissing along Amber's cheeks, making her way down to her neck, kissing along her collar bone and then down towards her chest, still holding one of Amber's wrists in her hand. "I'm only going to tie one up, so you're still free and able to do whatever you want. I just want it to seem like I'm having my way with you."

Amber doesn't even have anything to say to this. She's so turned on all over again, pressing her thighs together to create pressure between her legs, moaning and laying her head back on the pillow, letting Demi do just that, calling the shots and having her way with her.

Demi makes her way all the way up Amber's arm, kissing her all over, and then she slowly kisses the palm of her hand, and all Amber's fingertips, tasting herself on them. Then ever so slowly, she ties one of Amber's hands to the headboard of the bed, partially tying her up, restraining her.

She sits back for a moment and takes in the scene before her, this gorgeous, naked woman lying on the bed in front of her, half tied up, and hers for the taking. How the heck did this even happen to her, that this is the part she gets to play in their heist, and that it all worked out for her like this. She almost laughs out loud.

Instead she moves back between Amber's legs once more, and slowly leans down and licks her wet slit, pushing her tongue deep between her hot wet folds and making her way up to Amber's little clit, making her cry out once more. Then without skipping a beat, she reaches over and grabs the bottle of lube she left on the bed beside them, opens it up and pours some over her fingers. This time when she slides her fingers inside of Amber, they're slippery and wet with a texture so unlike her own juices, and it's so erotic and hot, that Amber moans out loud, pulling against the tie, thrusting her hips upwards into Demi's mouth and hand.

Demi wiggles her fingers around deep inside of Amber, finding her g-spot, and pressing on it hard while she continues to suck on Amber's clit, pulling it between her soft lips, twisting it around in her mouth. Demi slides her fingers almost all of the way out again, and this time when she slides them back inside she adds a third finger, feeling Amber slowly opening up to her.

Amber isn't going to take long to cum this time around, loving the feeling of Demi's slippery fingers sliding in and out of her, touching her in places she'd never been touched, opening her up, making her toes curl and her insides feel weak.

With her free hand she reaches down and runs her fingers through Demi's hair, grabbing on tightly, pulling her face in closer. She pushes herself up off the bed, her hips thrusting towards Demi's mouth, eager for more. Ready to cum. "Oh, are you going to cum already?" Demi asks in a purr, her voice vibrating on Amber's clit.

Amber can only moan in response, nodding her head, pulling against her restraint and grinding herself against Demi's hand. Demi picks up speed, fingering Amber harder, forcing her fingers deep inside her, rubbing her g-spot, and she hungerly laps at Amber's clit, pushing her over the edge.

Demi's listening to Amber's little cries and mews, loving the sounds she's making, when she swears she hears something else, another noise in the house, not coming from them in the bedroom. But whatever sound she heard is muffled a moment later as Amber wraps her thighs around Demi's shoulders, pulling her in closer as she starts to cum, crying out for her.

Moaning loudly, letting go of Demi's hair and reaching back for the sheets on the bed, pulling at them, grabbing at everything around her, Amber lets herself go, riding her orgasm, as Demi's tongue moves down through all her wetness and pushes its way deep into her hole, lapping up all her juices.

She doesn't stop this time though, like Amber assumes she would, and after a few more movements of tongue she feels Demi pull away and then two of her fingers slide back inside of her once more, pushing on her sweet spots while she is still so sensitive and coming down from that last orgasm, bringing her back up again.

Amber cries out from the sensations and opens her eyes to see Demi sitting between her legs, looking at her hungerly, watching her hand rub all over Amber's pussy. Her other hand is slowly making its way between her own legs, eager to feel good while she makes Amber feel good, again.

This is all too much for Amber, and she throws her sweaty body back down on the bed, spreading her legs wide, letting Demi have her way with her all over again. Amber's pussy is so wet and swollen from her juices and cum and the lube, that Demi's fingers slide in easily, and Amber cries out in ecstasy as Demi slides a third finger inside her again, opening her up again, spreading her wide.

Demi slides her own fingers up and down her wet slit, moaning in time with Amber, watching her fingers disappear again and again inside her pussy. Slowly, she pushes her own fingers inside herself at the same time, the feeling completely erotic, and she shudders, closing her eyes for a moment, enjoying fingering them both at once.

Using her thumb, she slowly slides it over Amber's clit, causing her to jump and moan, while slowly pushing her third finger in and out once more, opening her wider, watching Amber's wet pussy drip all over her hand. With the hand that's inside herself, she pushes back a bit, opening her hand up so that her palm rubs against her own clit, wiggling her fingers inside of herself, causing her to moan.

Now Demi is fingering them both in time with one another, both her hands working feverishly, fingers wiggling, pushing, rubbing. Amber's pussy is sopping wet, and the sounds her fingers make slipping in and out, mixed with both of their moans and mews and cries of enjoyment, fill the room.

Amber grips the sheets around her with her free hand, thrusting her hips up off the bed, loving being taken like this. She is already feeling so incredibly horny, and turned on, and still riding the waves of her last orgasm, and when she looks up again and watches Demi finger fuck herself while fingering her, it's enough to speed it up again.

Demi can tell that Amber is going to cum again soon, and she plans to cum right there with her. She is so turned on right now, Demi isn't sure if she's ever experienced anything so erotic in her entire life as this right now, taking them both at the same time, Amber tied to the bed. The two of them are moaning, almost in unison, and Demi picks up speed even more, hammering her fingers deep inside them both, rubbing circles around Amber's clit with her thumb while she grinds her own clit against the palm of her hand.

"Ooooohhhh," Amber lets out this deep throated growl, "I can't believe I'm going to cum again. Please, take me harder, don't stop, make me cum all over your fingers!" she cries out, bucking wildly underneath Demi's hand. Demi doesn't plan to, and she keeps going even though Amber is wiggling so hard all over the place that she almost wiggles out from underneath her and would have if she wasn't tied to the bed by one hand.

And Amber is yanking on that tie as she builds herself up, feeling it pull and bite into her wrist, loving the feeling of being immobile and unable to move while Demi has her way with her. They both get closer and closer to orgasm, the pair grinding into Demi's hands at the same time, crying out for more.

Amber is the first to cum, almost screaming out for more, bucking herself up off the bed as her orgasm overtakes her, and her tight pussy walls start to clench around Demi's fingers. Watching Amber's face change as she begins to cum, listening to her cries, feeling her wet folds tightening around Demi's hand, Amber's legs pulling her close, it's all too much for Demi and she begins to cum too, her cries mixing in with Amber's.

It takes them both a few minutes before their orgasms begin to subside, and their bodies stop trembling, and ever so slowly, Demi removes her hands from them both, and then collapses onto the bed beside Amber, breathing heavy, totally sexually spent.

"Wow," Amber whispers almost breathlessly, "that was unbelievable." Demi just laughs and curls up next to her, catching her breath, running her hands ever so slightly along Amber's smooth body, taking her in one last time. "That was so good, I could almost use a smoke, and I'm not even a smoker," Demi says with a laugh, to which Amber replies, "There's some in my husband's night stand, grab us one and we can share it."

Demi laughs and rolls over and grabs a smoke, a lighter and an ashtray from the drawer, feeling naughty, and sits back on the bed, getting comfortable beside Amber. Demi still hasn't untied her, but Amber hasn't made any move to do so herself either, having one hand free as well to do so. The two of them share the smoke, slowly passing it back and forth, not talking much, but still naked and cozied up to each other on the bed.

Demi is so lost in the moment, she could stay here all night. There is something about this woman that Demi just can't get enough of, and even after everything they have done together tonight, she wants more, she wants to make Amber cum over and over again until she's begging Demi to stop, and then she wants to make her cum some more.

But the reality of what's happening right now, what's already transpired tonight, is starting to catch up with her, and as she lays there, Demi finds herself wondering if Adam is done, if he's still in the house, if he heard that, if he saw any of that through the windows. She wonders what he's thinking now. Those thoughts are enough to send her mind spinning, and turn her stomach into knots, and she takes a deep breath, trying to mentally prepare herself for what's coming next.

The two of them slowly begin talking about what happens now for them, and Demi lets her know that once she's gained some feeling back in her legs, she's going to get herself dressed and head out, before she over stays her welcome. Amber offers to let her stay, reminding her that her husband isn't due home for another day or two, but as tempting as that is to Demi, she knows she can't stay, even if she would give the world to do so.

They kiss a few more times, soft bodies pressed against one another, Demi running her hands all over Amber's body one last time but stopping herself before she ends up getting Amber too worked up again. Slowly, ever so slowly, she pulls herself away from Amber, and the bed, and begins to get dressed.

She offers to untie Amber, but Amber shakes her head, laughing. "Nah, you can leave me this way, I don't mind. I can untie myself later, and for now, it's kind of a nice reminder. I wouldn't mind the TV remote from over there on the dresser though." She says, pointing with her free hand.

Demi walks over and retrieves the remote, now fully dressed herself, and she walks back over to the bed as Amber is sliding her slender, naked body underneath the covers. Once again, she finds herself regretting this decision to leave. She hands Amber the remote and helps her slide underneath the bedspread, tucking her in almost, and then she leans down and kisses her one last time, unable to help herself. Amber's lips are still so soft, and gentle, and she tastes wine and herself on Amber's lips, still lingering from earlier. Damn, she thinks to herself, how badly she wants to stay.

Once they finally break away from their kiss, Demi walks back over to the dresser and leaves a fake cell phone number on the pad of paper there, even though it kills her to do so. Amber asked for her number, and she couldn't just say no after everything that had gone down, nor could she give her real number either.

They both share a laugh again, at how crazy this whole situation had been, about how nice it was to spend time together that evening, and getting to know one another, and about how it hadn't really ever been weird, or awkward at all, just really nice. Then with a deep breath, Demi leaves, letting herself out the bedroom and then through the house, taking one last look around as she goes, everything feeling surreal.

Then she lets herself out the front door, shutting and locking it behind her, and slowly she makes her way down the walkway, back towards the road, and where Adam is supposed to be parked and waiting for her, feeling like she's in a dream world.

Chapter Twenty

Demi walks down the street slowly, making her way back towards the meeting spot where Adam will have parked the car, in a total daze. Her emotions are absolutely all over the map, and she's finding it hard to keep anything straight, or know what she's really supposed to be feeling now that all of this is over, at least for her.

Part of her is still feeling drunk from the wine, and high from her sexual experience with Amber. It had been unlike anything she's ever been through before in her life, let alone with another woman. It had been exciting, and fun, thrilling, scary, and such a turn on, all at the same time. When she did remember about Adam, and what they were really there for, she felt such a rush at the thought of being seen, of being watched, of him knowing everything she'd done to Amber.

But then again, another part of her feels guilty, and unsure, because there were a few moments when she had forgotten about him, and the heist entirely, and she doesn't know if he did see anything, what he thought about it, or what he feels about the whole thing anyway, and about her being with Amber. Now that all of this is over, she is kicking herself for never having had that discussion with him in the first place. It seems a whole lot more important now than the history of the house, or any of the other dumb things they'd spoke about instead.

As she walks, the car begins to appear in the distance on the side of the road, although it's parked in a very dark spot on the street, and hard to make out. She can't tell if Adam is in the car yet, if he's back from the heist, but from the look of the sky, it's far later, or earlier in the morning, then she had imagined, and the likely hood is if all went well, he has been waiting for her for a while.

The closer she gets to the car, the more her thoughts begin to jump and jumble, and her heart begins to race and hammer in her chest. She can't help stressing and wondering what his reaction is going to be to all of this, and she's worried what kind of an effect this whole thing is going to have on their still developing relationship, especially if this isn't something that's settling well with him. What if he's upset with her, or doesn't trust her anymore?

As she reaches the front of the car, it turns on, lights brightening the road behind her, and she almost stumbles, so started by the sound of the engine. She opens the door and gets in a little hesitantly, and the car is silent, with Adam not saying a word to her, or even looking at her. So, she doesn't say anything either, and as she sits down and starts to shut the door, Adam begins to drive off, before she's even had a chance to put on her seatbelt.

Now she can't help but be concerned about the situation. She takes her eyes off of Adam, who hasn't stopped looking at the road ahead as he drives, and she glances into the backseat. There is nothing there, no bags, no black sack, and she feels a pit form in the bottom of her stomach. Was all of this for nothing? She thinks to herself.

"Relax babe, everything is in the trunk. Everything, and then some." He says with a small laugh, and Demi can't quite read the tone of his voice. "But we need to change plans, right now. We're going back to the hotel and clearing out and hitting the road, as fast as we can."

If Demi thought her heart was racing before, it's running a marathon now, so unsure of what's happening with the heist, what's happening right now, and what's happening between them. She wants to ask, but there is something about his posture, something about the way he's driving, knuckles white on the steering wheel, desperate to get to the hotel, that makes her keep silent, staring out the window as the late-night street lights fly by, biting her lip.

Eventually, they get to the hotel, and Adam parks at the bottom of the stairs to the landing where their room is. He doesn't turn off the car, instead, he turns and looks at her and says "I can't come in with you. I need to stay with the car, just in case. I want you to go in and get everything. All our stuff. Just throw it into suitcases and bring it out. I don't want you to miss anything, but I don't want you to worry about packing it neat and tidy either. Just get our shit, and get it fast please babe, and get back out here so we can go. Hurry."

Demi gets out of the car, feeling lost, and like she's walked out of the jeweler's house and into the twilight zone. Or maybe that happened before she even got there. Nothing has seemed real since she walked up the pathway to the house earlier tonight and knocked on the door. She hustles her way up into their hotel room and begins throwing all their stuff together into bags. Her mind is racing, wondering, questioning, but she doesn't have any answers and doesn't know if Adam is going to provide any right now anyway.

She has a final look around the room, under the beds and in the bathroom, making sure that she's gotten everything they own, and then she grabs their bags and hurries out of the room, letting the door lock behind her and dragging their stuff down the hall. Luckily, we travel light, she thinks bitterly to herself, unable to help the unsettled and yucky way that she's feeling.

She races back down the stairs towards the car, finding Adam standing outside of the driver's door, arms crossed, waiting for her. She still can't read the expression on his face, and she's driving herself mad trying to figure out what's going on. As soon as she draws close enough, he grabs the bags from her and throws them in the back seat, leaving her free to get back into the car.

"I didn't want to leave the car," he says to her as he grabs them, and it makes her wonder again, how exactly did the heist go? What did he see? And how is he feeling about all of this now?

Demi shuts the door and buckles her seatbelt, and Adam climbs in, starting the car. He doesn't say another word to her, he simply checks behind them and then drives off, heading out onto the highway and driving east, away from the city.

Chapter Twenty-One

The silence in the car feels deafening, roaring in her ears. Adam may be lost in his own thoughts, but she can't stand the quiet any more, she can't take the feelings jumbling around inside of her, and she hates how she feels absolutely sick to her stomach right now and doesn't even really know why. She can't be alone with her thoughts anymore.

The farther they drive away from the city, the more Demi's anxiety and tension grows, and eventually, she feels like she's about to snap. Instead, she forces herself to take a long, slow deep breath, and starts by asking him if the heist went well.

To this, Adam starts to laugh. And it's not a small, awkward laugh but a big, deep belly laugh, as if her question wasn't a question at all, but some hilarious inside joke that she's not a part of, the funniest one of all. It startles her, catching her totally off guard. She didn't know what she had been expecting, but it definitely isn't for him to break out into a fit of laughter at her question.

Adam keeps laughing as he begins to slow the car down and he switches lanes, waiting for an exit sign to appear. They are in the middle of nowhere right now, and that suits him perfectly. Demi finds herself wondering if Adam is in a bad mood at all, he certainly doesn't seem to be. His laughter and attitude are throwing her off, and she hates that even with all this time that they've spent together, she still has a hard time reading his expressions and his body language.

"Well, the heist went great. Too great. It was fantastic babe, holy shit." He says with a laugh. Then, after checking all the mirrors, he slowly pulls the car off at the next exit, and then heads them down a couple of back roads, leading them off the highway and somewhere they can talk quietly. With everything that's happened, he can't help but feel a twinge of paranoia, even though he doesn't think there's really a need for it.

As they're driving to what feels like the middle of nowhere, Demi can't help but feel her emotions flying all over the place, unsure of what she should really feel. Why is he laughing? If the heist went well, what is all this midnight rush about? She's feeling so confused, and worn out from the drink, and the late nights they've been keeping, and all the anxiety she's feeling. Plus, she still has this ache between her legs, lingering, leftover from her time with Amber, and that thought sends her into a whole other whirlwind of emotions on top of it all.

Eventually, they get to a place that Adam feels is secluded enough, and he pulls the car over and then parks, shutting off the engine and unbuckling his seatbelt. He turns to face her, and even though his face is still unreadable, there is a gleam of excitement in his eyes that gives him away.

"Demi, the heist really did go fantastic," he says. "You have no idea how much, well, how much everything, we are driving around with in the trunk right now. My buddy was way off on what was really being kept in that place, or the jeweler has been adding to it, and even after Joes cut, wow. Just wow. Except now I'm so paranoid, I just want us to dump this off, stat. I don't want to be driving around with it. I want us to take our cut, our money, whatever we want out of it, and just go. I want us to be so long gone from this place, rolling in the big bucks, before her husband ever even comes home and knows that he's been robbed. Or that you weren't who you were claiming to be either."

He takes a deep breath and continues. "And by the way, oh my god Demi, wow. You almost gave me a damn heart attack, what a fucking delicious scene that was to walk past mid robbery. So damn hot, I almost dropped everything I was doing and came in my fucking pants."

Demi catches him looking at her with that gleam in his eyes again, and she thinks over everything he's just said to her, letting out a huge breath she didn't even notice she'd been holding for a while. "So, you're not mad, or upset about what I did?" She asks in a little voice, nervous to ask still, but needing to ask all the same, needing to finally know how he feels.

Adam doesn't answer right away. Instead, he leans forward, taking her face in his hands, kissing her so deeply, so passionately that her toes curl. His touch is so much firmer, and stronger, with so much more authority on her body compared to Amber's. She moans into his mouth, as his hands make their way all over her body, and that ache begins to stir between her legs again, as if she hasn't already been satisfied enough tonight.

She starts kissing him back eagerly, so glad to be in his arms again, so glad that they feel ok, even if he hasn't said as much yet. She can feel his breathing speed up, and he shifts in his seat, clearly getting excited from their kissing, and from the scene he's replaying in his mind.

"Damn it Demi, as badly as I just want to pull you into my lap and fuck you right now, we can't. We have got to get out of here, get to the next drop spot, get rid of some of this stuff and go on our way. I'll feel a whole lot better then. And a lot less distracted, so I can have my way with you the way I want."

He takes a deep breath, steadying himself, thinking over the next part of the plan. "I'm going to drive us straight on through until morning, making up as much time as possible on the empty highways, and try to get us to the next place with a little bit of time to spare, just to be safe. You are *not* coming with me, there is absolutely no way I would ever take that risk. I'm going to drop you off at a hotel, and you can check in, let me know the room number, and get yourself settled. Maybe have a shower or get some sleep, eat something, whatever you want to do. I shouldn't be more than an hour or two, and I'll be coming back to you with enough money to make us very, very, *very* rich. And then you are going to be all mine."

Demi laughs, feeling relieved about everything now that they've really had a chance to talk. And suddenly, she's also feeling very sleepy, and a little drunk still, or maybe on the verge of a hangover, all that wine and sexual fun getting to her now, wearing her out, the excitement of the evening gone.

Adam laughs too, starting the car again, and then he reaches over and takes her hand as he starts to drive back towards the highway. "Why don't you get some sleep, we have a long drive ahead of us, and you look exhausted," Adam says, and she nods, too tired to argue, lifting her feet up onto the seat, reclining it a little bit and getting as comfortable as the seatbelt will allow her to.

It doesn't take her more than a few minutes and she is sleeping soundly, propped up with her head against the window, her hand still tucked into Adam's. He sneaks glances at her as he drives, amused at the small smile on her face that she's fallen asleep with, feeling his heart swell with love for her.

He can't help but think to himself that everything went so incredibly well, and he wouldn't have been able to pull all that off without her. He slowly removes his hand from hers as he drives, and slides it into his pocket, feeling the ring that he'd stolen and tucked away inside, thinking about their future, and what's going to be in store for them next.

Chapter Twenty-Two

Demi wakes up with the rising sun in her eyes, the feeling of the car's engine still rumbling beneath her. Her whole body is stiff and sore, and slowly she stretches, realizing she's been sleeping tucked into a ball against the door for the better part of the night. All of her muscles scream in protest, never mind her head, which is pounding with a full-blown wine hangover.

She looks around out the window and sees that they're pulling into another city, in a whole other state. Taking a glance over at Adam, still perched behind the wheel driving, she notices that he looks absolutely dead exhausted. She feels a wave of guilt pour over her, realizing she's been sleeping this entire time and never offered to drive, but then again, she'd been drinking the night before and been too drunk. The thumping in her head reminds her of that.

"We are almost at the hotel I googled a little while ago, trying to find the closest one," Adam says, once he notices she's awake. "I'm going to drop you off in a few minutes like I said last night, and I just want you to go in and relax and not worry about anything. Have a shower, sleep some more, get yourself some coffee and something to eat, whatever you want. I won't be long, I promise."

Demi listens to his words, half asleep, wondering to herself why he's repeated the plan so many times, is he trying to reassure her, or himself? She's not coherent enough to ask though, as her head is throbbing, and not just from the wine, so she sits back in her seat and watches the city appear out her window as they draw closer to the outskirts and the nearest hotel.

When they reach the hotel, Adam pulls into the parking lot and parks the car, but he doesn't shut it off, in that much of a hurry to drop her off and get out of here and dump the stolen goods. He does lean in and kiss her goodbye, but he's distracted, and it's not much more than a peck on her lips. Demi doesn't even mind, still feeling disoriented and slightly out of it, and she simply grabs her bags and gets out of the car, watching him drive off.

As she walks towards the hotel office, she wonders what any possible people watching her might make of her current situation. Probably think I'm a hooker, dropped off after a night shift, she thinks to herself with a laugh, and then pushes the thought aside. She knows exactly what's going on, and that's all that matters.

Demi wanders into the office and checks in, getting a room for two and the keys. She makes her way to the room, sets her bags down, and then sits down on the bed, pulling out her phone. She sends Adam a text with the room number, and then sets it down on the dresser, knowing she's not going to get a response, but wanting one anyway.

Then she lays back on the bed, taking in a deep breath and holding it for a few seconds before letting all the air in her lungs out in one long whoosh, staring up at the ugly hotel ceiling. Slowly, she wills her mind to relax and to stop spinning, now that everything is said and done. Her part is over, she will never see the wife again, everything seems fine between her and Adam, even though his part isn't done, and eventually he'll be back, they can settle down together, and everything will go back to normal, right? Demi tries to reassure herself, but she can't quite shake the knot that's still tied in the pit of her stomach.

Despite her best efforts, many of the events of the last 48 hours begin to play and replay through her mind on repeat, the good ones and the bad. The more she tries not to think about them, the more she does, and the more her mind begins to drift and wander, now that she's alone, in the peace and quiet of the hotel room, without any stress or pressure.

And then, as her mind begins to drift, Demi feels herself start to drift away as well, still feeling sleepy from the whirlwind of the last few days on the go. She snaps herself awake and forces herself to get up and get moving, determined not to fall asleep right now. She checks the time and is startled to see that it's already been over an hour since she'd gotten here. Time flies when you're tired, she thinks with a laugh.

She starts a pot of coffee in the little mini kitchen area of the room, and then drags herself into the shower, turning the water up as hot as she can take it, letting it wake her up a bit. She takes her time, washing her hair slowly, then soaping herself up, feeling almost as if she's trying to rinse everything away that she's been through, so that she can start over clean.

The smell of cheap hotel coffee brewing in the other room is strong, and it overpowers the smell of shampoo and soap, perking her up even more. She finishes up her shower, hopping out and drying herself off, throwing a towel in her hair turban style to dry. Then she wraps another towel around her body and heads back out into the main room, to make herself a cup.

Just as she's standing there putting her coffee together, there is a knock at the door, and her heart stops in her chest. She isn't sure what to do, standing there in only a towel, wondering if it's Adam at the door, or possibly someone else, someone who knew what they were up to. Then the knocking comes again, urgently, and she makes a decision, rushing over to the door and peeking out through the peephole.

There she finds Adam almost jumping from foot to foot, pacing in anticipation for her to open the door. Something about the look on his face has her worried sick, and she unlocks the door and throws it wide, greeting him in only a towel, about to ask him what's wrong.

Adam pushes past her and before she can get a word out, he grabs her around the waist, pulling her into him, and reaches around her and slams the door shut, locking both the door and the deadbolt behind him. Then he pushes them both up against the wall, the feeling both cool and erotic on her hot, still wet skin. He drops a large duffle bag and a briefcase down on the floor beside them, things she hadn't even noticed he'd been carrying, and then suddenly his lips are on hers, all over her, kissing her deeply.

His hands are on her body, all over her, and he starts pulling at her towel, trying to remove it from around her.

Demi attempts to end their kiss, trying to break away so that she can talk to him for a second, but he is relentless, with his mouth and tongue all over hers, needing to have her.

Demi has a million and one questions for him, her brain still going a mile a minute, and desperate for answers now that he's finally here in front of her, and it's all over, but he won't let her ask them yet. Instead, he forces her hands away from her body, opening her to him. Then he grasps onto the edge of her towel and rips of off of her in one smooth motion, leaving her naked and wet in front of him, totally exposed, shivering from the cold and the anticipation.

She can't help but let out a loud moan, totally caught off guard. Adam looks at her hungerly, taking in every inch of her from the top of her head right down to the tip of her toes, loving her tight wet body. Adam uses his knee and pushes her legs apart, opening her up completely while still pinning her against the cool hotel room wall.

Then suddenly, Adam is on the floor in front of her, hands on the outsides of her spread open thighs. He leans forward, and his mouth is on her hot pussy, devouring her. She gasps and withers against the wall as he reaches up and uses his fingers to spread her lips wide, exposing her hot folds. Then his tongue is everywhere, licking and sucking on her, sliding his tongue inside of her, tasting her, wanting more.

Demi moans again loudly, loving the feel of Adam's mouth all over her. She lifts up one of her legs, placing her slender calf on Adam's shoulder, opening herself up even more, letting him take her. Adam uses this new position to his advantage and pushes two of his fingers deep inside Demi, wiggling them around, touching all of her sweet spots. His tongue continues to lick and suck on her clit, determined to bring her to an orgasm right there against the wall.

Adam picks up speed with his fingers, pushing them deeper and deeper inside Demi, rubbing against her g-spot, making her cry out as her thigh clenches around his shoulder, pulling him close. He laughs a little at her eagerness, at how willing her body is responding to him, and the vibrations send shudders through her and make her gasp loudly, reminding her of her time with Amber, turning her on even more.

It isn't going to take her long, and she lets him know, reaching down and taking his head in her hands, pulling him tightly between her legs, anxious for more, dying to cum on his face, in his mouth.

Adam wants to taste her just as badly as he's ready to bury himself inside of her. He rubs her g-spot again roughly, wiggling his fingers inside her as he takes her clit into his mouth, twirling his tongue around it. She cries out as her orgasm takes her over the edge, clinging to him as her body shakes, her pussy clenching and squeezing around his fingers, her juices pouring down his hand.

He doesn't stop until she's completely done, not able to get enough of her. He keeps licking every last drop until her body stops shaking and her breathing slows down, and he feels her hands loosen their grip on his head.

When he feels like she's finally done, he slides backwards a bit and stands up, grabbing her tightly around the waist. Then he picks her up, while she squeals and grabs onto him, and he carries her over to the bed, tossing her naked body down on the comforter.

Slowly he starts to strip off his clothes, as he watches her body on the bed, breaking out in goosebumps, still chilly and wet from her shower. "You have no idea how rich we are right now Demi," he says to her, throwing his shirt off and then working on his pants. "We just pulled off the hottest, most incredible, jewelry and money heist ever. Ever. It was so easy, so worth it, and oh, yes, so very hot."

Adam climbs up on the bed, and covers her naked body with his own, his hot skin warming her instantly as he starts to kiss and lick and touch her everywhere, not able to get enough of her. "And it was easy because of you, you know." He continues between nibbles on her breasts. "You were so incredibly sexy, what a turn on that was. Did you have any idea that I was watching from the doorway for part of that, watching you take you both while you had her tied to the bed?"

Demi doesn't say anything to this, she just moans, laying back on the bed and letting Adam have his way with her, the way she'd had her way with Amber, feeling so incredibly turned knowing that he had been watching her with Amber, and loving what he had seen.

His hands and mouth are still all over her body, driving her crazy, and now she can feel his rock-hard cock pressed up against her leg, pressing into her, his pre-cum oozing out and leaving a trail along her thigh as he moves his body against hers.

"Oh, what I would have done to be able to come in that room with the two of you, tie you up right along with her, and have my way with you both. Take you robber style." Demi groans loudly at the thought of this, her pussy flooding with juices, and she thrusts her hips up against Adam, eager for more, eager to feel him inside of her.

Adam keeps talking, telling her all the things he wishes he could have done to her, and Amber, while sliding his cock up and down her wet slit, driving her crazy, turning her on more and more. She's twisting and squirming on the bed underneath him now, clinging to him, all but begging him to bury his cock inside of her and fuck her until she cums.

"Babe, you're so wet," he says as his cock slides down between her folds one last time, and then he thrusts his hips forward, filing her all the way to the bottom, the head of his cock hitting the walls of her vagina, causing her to cry out into him. "All this naughty talk must turn you on." He slides his cock almost all the way back out before slamming inside her again, watching her face change as she moans. "Maybe I'll have to tie you up and fuck you hard while I rob *you* of all your millions one day."

He picks up speed, giving it to her roughly, holding her tightly while she clings to him just as hard, wrapping her legs around his waist, pulling him into her and matching his thrusts with her hips, grinding hard against him.

It isn't going to take either of them long to orgasm, both so desperate for one another, and so turned on by the events of the night before, and all the dirty things Adam has been talking about doing. He leans down and kisses her again, pushing his tongue deeply into her mouth, rubbing her tongue with his in time with his cock thrusting inside of her.

She moans into his mouth, her nails digging into his back, crying out for more. Her pussy begins to tighten around him, milking him, driving him wild as she starts to orgasm, her body trembling underneath him. The feeling of her silky folds tightening around his cock over and over sets him off, and they orgasm together, hot, sweaty, clinging to each other as they kiss and moan.

They hold each other, naked still, breathing heavy and hearts racing, as they come down, just enjoying the moment. "I love you, " Adam says into her ear, pulling her close, and Demi replies in kind, pushing her body back against his, snuggling up even closer.

Then Adam lets out a huge yawn, his whole body shaking, as exhaustion sets in and he realizes just how tired he really is, having pulled more than an all nighter, and having drove for hours, on top of all the stress and excitement and anxiety of the heist.

"I'm about to pass out love," Adam says sleepily, pulling her even closer. "Let me get a couple hours of shut eye, and then when I wake up, we can get human again, and you and I are going to hit the road." "Where are we going now hun?" Demi asks, not really sure if she'll get an answer, as Adam is already starting to breath heavy, and his eyes are closed.

"Wherever you want babe," he replies with a yawn a few moments later, "Let's travel the world together. We're so rich, we can go anywhere we want. But maybe, let's start with finding you another bored sexy housewife to seduce."

Demi laughs at this, feeling content and in love and sleepy herself, and she wraps her arms around him, listening to him snore softly as she drifts away into sleep, thinking about the future, and all the possibilities it holds for them.

The End… of Book 2

Thank you from the bottom of my heart to each and every one of you who have supported me this far!
Please stay tuned for Book #3… Due out by Christmas 2018

Made in the USA
Middletown, DE
25 June 2020